"TO GO INTO THE BLACK JUNGLE," TABAQUI SAID, "IS TO INVITE DEATH."

"Unless one is knowing the way," Buldeo said.

"The jungle boy," Wilkins said.

"Precisely," Boone said. He took the dagger away from Buldeo, carefully wrapped it, and hid it again in his vest. "But getting Mowgli's cooperation will take some—how to put this delicately?—persuasion."

Buldeo and Tabaqui grinned unpleasantly at each other, showing many rotted teeth. "Have no fear, sahib,' Buldeo said. "I am having all the persuasion you need."

The Jungle Book

A novelization by

MEL GILDEN

based on the script by Stephen Sommers
and Ron Yanover & Mark Geldman
based on the novel by Rudyard Kipling

HarperPaperbacks
A Division of HarperCollinsPublishers

This is a work of fiction. The characters, incidents, and dialogues are products of the author's imagination and are not to be construed as real. Any resemblance to actual events or persons, living or dead, is entirely coincidental.

HarperPaperbacks   *A Division of* HarperCollins*Publishers*
10 East 53rd Street, New York, N.Y. 10022

Copyright © 1994 by Vegahom Europe BV.
All rights reserved. No part of this book may be used or reproduced in any manner whatsoever without written permission of the publisher, except in the case of brief quotations embodied in critical articles and reviews. For information address HarperCollins*Publishers*,
10 East 53rd Street, New York, N.Y. 10022.

Cover and photo insert © 1994 Buena Vista Distribution, Inc. and Vegahom Europe BV.

Insert photography by Frank Connor

First HarperPaperbacks printing: December 1994

Printed in the United States of America

HarperPaperbacks and colophon are trademarks of HarperCollins*Publishers*

❖ 10 9 8 7 6 5 4 3

Contents

For Jack Favere—
The Man Who Would Be King

The Jungle Book

1

Major Brydon's Caravan

Now these are the Laws of the Jungle, and many and mighty are they;
But the head and the hoof of the Law and the haunch and the hump is—Obey!
                                    —FROM THE JUNGLE LAW
                                    AS SPOKEN BY BALOO

It has been said, O best beloved, that life is a spinning wheel, with each spoke a tale to be told. So keep silence along the banks, and I will tell you a story as enchanting as the Indian jungle itself: a tale of long ago, when your grandfather traveled across the jungles of India with your mother, who in the time I am speaking of was nearly as young and fresh as you are yourself.

1

Some of it I saw myself, and some I was told later.

The tale I tell is about pride and power and treasure, about fangs and claws and talons. But mostly, O best beloved, it is about love.

So listen well, and hear the call. And good hunting to those who keep the Jungle Law!

Once, there was a she-wolf named Raksha, and she had four bold wolf pups. Her favorite was the boldest of them all, a pup with a large white smudge on his forehead. In later times he would be known as Gray Brother.

As he did often, Gray Brother ran away from the safe cave where his brothers and sisters still romped. He ran into the jungle, paying no attention to the roars of Shere Khan, the great tiger who was hunting thereabouts.

Raksha soon noticed that Gray Brother was gone, and with fear in her heart, she went to search for him.

And indeed, Shere Khan picked up Gray Brother's scent, and stalked him while thinking of the tasty morsel the wolf pup would make.

Gray Brother heard his mother's howl behind him and the growl of Shere Khan before him. He stood where he was, too frightened to move. The dense jungle leaves were suddenly thrust aside, and Gray Brother looked up, certain that he had lived his last moment on earth.

Into the tiny clearing stepped a five-year-old boy. He was strong and straight and nut-brown from the sun. When he saw the cringing wolf pup, his heart opened to it immediately, and he crouched down and peered at it wide-eyed and without fear. The pup peered back, as curious about the boy as the boy was about him. The boy heard someone enter the clearing behind him.

The man who entered the clearing was the brave and reliable Nathoo, a guide for the British, and the father of Mowgli, the small boy. No one knew more about the plants and animals of the Indian jungle than Nathoo.

"Look, Father," the boy said.

"He has lost his mother, Mowgli, just like you," Nathoo said as he reached down for the cub. It was a healthy male, and made a pleasant furry weight in his hands. The cub was seemingly as fearless as Mowgli. "Protect him with your life," Nathoo said as he handed the cub to his son, "and he will protect you with his."

"I will protect him, Father," Mowgli said as he stroked Gray Brother's soft fur.

Shere Khan watched this tender scene with great interest, but because he was on the far side of a wide river he could do nothing to stop his hunger. He merely growled.

Neither Mowgli nor his father knew of Shere Khan's presence until somewhat later. They returned to the caravan the British had formed to take Major Brydon (that's *me*, O best beloved) to his new post—a place at the edge of the world, surrounded by a million miles of jungle. Nathoo walked alongside the lead elephant, which due to its rank was painted all over in bright colors. In a howdah—which is like a little house—atop the lead elephant was Major Brydon himself, sweating and cursing the heat, and a little sick from the unfamiliar rolling motion of the elephant.

"Damned elephant! Get in line," Major Brydon called, but to no effect. The elephant continued to do exactly as it pleased.

All down both sides of the caravan marched British soldiers, as hot and itchy as their major. Each of them carried a rifle, which in this heat seemed no more than a dead weight.

At the rear of the procession—which is a very

4

grand parade—were rickety old carts drawn by Brahma bulls. The carts carried furniture and clothing, all the heavy British household possessions of Major Brydon and his daughter.

His daughter was in the cart just behind the last elephant, which was a baby. Mowgli sat atop the baby elephant cradling Gray Brother in his arms. The name of Major Brydon's daughter was Katherine, but everyone called her Kitty, even the servants, which Major Brydon thought too familiar by half, but Kitty did not seem to mind, so he said nothing about it.

Long before they met, from the moment they were born, Mowgli and Kitty had a common bond, for both their mothers had left this world while bringing them into it.

For now neither Kitty nor Mowgli was aware of the other's existence. They were fascinated by what Nathoo could do with his machete. He twirled it as if it were a baton and it flashed when it caught the sun. A group of pretty young Indian girls giggled and pointed as they watched. Suddenly Nathoo swung the machete down and slashed up a red flower that had been growing beside the path. The flower flew through the air and landed in the hands of the most beautiful

Indian girl. Nathoo leaned in and stole a kiss before giving a courtly bow.

The girls giggled even more as they ran to the back of the caravan, where they could study the flower and discuss the meaning of the kiss.

A tiger's roar rang across the jungle vastness, causing the elephants to brake ranks, and the painted elephant on which Major Brydon rode to rear up, nearly throwing him off, howdah and all. The bulls bellowed, and flocks of birds rose into the air with a great whoosh.

"Control yourself, you bloody elephant," the major cried. "Whoa! Whoa! I say!" But the elephant was too frightened to remember its training.

2

The Attack of Shere Khan

While Major Brydon was thrown up and back like a sailor in rough seas, Mowgli leapt in front of the elephant. "Tut-tut-tut!" Mowgli cried as he clapped his hands.

The elephant fell back to all fours, and its trunk tickled Mowgli's tummy, making him laugh. Both Kitty and her father were impressed by Mowgli's skill in handling animals.

"Buldeo! What on earth is going on?" Brydon called down to another of the guides, this one a rough-looking individual with an arrogant manner.

"Shere Khan," Buldeo called up to Brydon. "He has returned."

"Shere?" Brydon asked, more than a little worried. "A tiger?"

"Shere *Khan. King* of the tigers."

Major Brydon swept the jungle with his eyes, looking for a sign of the tiger, but he saw none. He knew only concern for his command, his house, and most of all for his young daughter. He did not know then that as surely as Shere Khan was to be the jungle's royal keeper, so Mowgli was destined to become its lord.

"Shere Khan is angry because men with guns have come to his jungle," Nathoo said, staring pointedly at Buldeo. "They come and they kill more than they can eat."

Buldeo shrugged. "What does a tiger care about a few animals more or less?" he asked.

"Would you allow someone to break into your house and steal your food?" Nathoo replied angrily.

Buldeo said nothing, but his disgust for Nathoo was unmistakable.

"Shere Khan knows you broke the Jungle Law," Nathoo went on. "He will surely stay close and watch for a chance to avenge himself."

"Welcome to India, Major Brydon," the major grumbled to himself while he watched the guides and soldiers trying to right carts and calm animals.

As if such things as tigers did not concern him, Mowgli swung himself back aboard his baby elephant. "Do not worry, memsab," he called over his shoulder to Kitty. "I will protect you."

"I will protect myself, thank you."

"What is your name?" Mowgli asked. As young as he was, he recognized beauty when he saw it.

"Kitty Brydon," she said. She was a very self-possessed little girl, and not the least bit shy. Though she was just as new to India as her father, from the moment she arrived she felt as if she belonged there. When she said that she could protect herself, she was not just boasting. She was stating the facts as she knew them.

"I am Mowgli," he said, and shrugged. He had no last name and had never needed one. "Just Mowgli."

He felt it necessary to impress Kitty then, perhaps to make up for the lack of a last name, perhaps because he recognized beauty when he saw it. Whatever his reasons, he pulled his own machete from his belt and began to wave it around, hoping to give the impression that he was as expert with it as his father. It slipped out of his hand, and when he tried to catch it, he reached too far and fell from the back of his elephant to the ground. Kitty could not help laughing. Mowgli's embarrassment was more painful than the bump he'd received.

Late that night the camp was peaceful. Around one fire the guides were telling stories of Rikki-Tikki-Tavi the mongoose, and Toomai of the elephants. Around another, the British soldiers talked of England, and of those who had been left behind. Exhausted, Major Brydon at last fell asleep despite being preyed upon by millions of bugs he could barely see. "Damned elephants," he grumbled in his sleep, confusing the elephants with the bugs.

Mowgli stood at the flap of the tent he shared with Nathoo, swaying to the music that floated across from the tent Kitty shared with her Indian nanny. He did not know it was a waltz, but he could feel the entrancing tug of its rhythm, a tug that generations of dancers had not been able to ignore. Kitty's shadow moved up and down the short length of the tent as she danced. In his hand, Mowgli held a red flower like the one his father had given to the beautiful Indian girl. Kitty's dancing and the flower's fragrance filled him with longing that he had no idea how to satisfy.

Then to his surprise and delight, Kitty twirled out of her tent and across the compound. Seeing his opportunity, Mowgli stepped forward, thus putting himself directly in her path. She stopped before she ran into him, embarrassed. He offered the flower to her and smiled as she took it. While she inhaled the flower's perfume Mowgli, copying his father again, closed his eyes and leaned in for a kiss.

He was very surprised when he received not a kiss, but a sock in the jaw! Mowgli's eyes snapped open to see that Kitty was as surprised by her actions as he was. Still gripping the flower, she quickly retreated into her tent.

Mowgli watched her go, trying to figure out what he'd done wrong. He did not know that men older and wiser than he had been trying to answer such questions for centuries without success. He was about to go to bed when to his surprise, Kitty leaned out of her tent and motioned to him. Despite his fear of another attack, Mowgli went to her. She took a bracelet from her own wrist and snapped it around Mowgli's. She then smiled at him warmly, blew him a kiss across her upturned palm, and ducked back inside.

Mowgli was stunned but happy. He went back into his own tent, feeling a little goofy. Nathoo was still awake, sharpening his machete on a big stone. Neither of them mentioned the bracelet, but Gray Brother sniffed at it and play-fully tried to worry it off Mowgli's wrist.

On a nearby table was a vase with some of the local flowers in it. Mowgli did not know how old the vase was, certainly older than himself, for he could not remember a time when Nathoo was without it. It was covered with pictures of animals, and Nathoo used the vase to teach him the animals' names in both their native language and in English. Mowgli knew that *baloo* meant bear, and that *bagheera* meant panther, and that *kaa* meant snake.

Nathoo turned the vase, bringing a tiger into Mowgli's sight. The tiger had a crack across his middle and a chunk of him was missing, but he was a fearsome beast nonetheless.

"That is me," Mowgli said.

"You?" Nathoo said. He stopped sharpening his machete to look at Mowgli.

"The holy man says I am half-tiger."

"Half a tiger?" Nathoo asked, somewhat confused.

"Holy man says that when I face Shere Khan and show no fear, I will be a whole tiger."

Nathoo did not know what to make of any of this. The truth was, Mowgli's talk frightened him a little. And Nathoo was not a man who frightened easily. "Where did you see this holy man?"

"In my dreams," Mowgli said, as if dreaming of holy men was as common as rain during the wet season.

Before Nathoo could ask more questions, the camp exploded into chaos. The quiet night was broken by rifle shots, people running and shouting, and animals shrieking in terror. Nathoo grabbed his machete and ran out. Mowgli thrust Gray Brother down inside his shirt for safety, and followed.

Major Brydon, rifle in hand, was kneeling next to a soldier. He turned and saw something that horrified him. Mowgli looked where the major was looking and saw a big tiger loping toward Buldeo. Buldeo was petrified with fear.

Mowgli was sure the tiger was Shere Khan, and that he was here to exact his revenge against Buldeo for killing more than he could eat.

Nathoo leapt between Buldeo and Shere Khan, his machete poised as a weapon. Shere Khan hesitated for a moment, then leapt at Nathoo. Nathoo spun away, but Shere Khan caught him on the shoulder and the machete went flying. It stuck in the dirt still quivering, and far out of reach of any of the men. Mowgli knew what he must do.

"Get back, memsab!" he called to Kitty as he rushed past her tent.

In another moment Mowgli swooped up the machete. "Bapu!" he called as he tossed it to his father.

Nathoo caught the machete and swung it around, slicing Shere Khan across one cheek. The tiger roared with pain and anger, and ran off. Knowing that he was safe for the moment, Nathoo went to help calm the pack animals.

Mowgli climbed onto a nearby cart to get a better view of the entertainment—for any excitement is entertaining to a young boy, no matter how serious it may be. The horses hitched to it nervously pawed the earth, tossed their heads, and whinnied. The cart had a few barrels in it, and he sat down atop one of them. Gray Brother peered out from his collar, wide-eyed.

People were running every which way, like ants when their homes are disturbed. Somewhere nearby, Shere Khan continued to roar. A goat ran by, crying out most piteously.

Major Brydon stood across the clearing with a rifle in his hands. At the same time he and Mowgli saw Shere Khan enter the clearing. The major shot at Shere Khan, but missed, hitting instead a kerosene lamp hanging like an orange in the doorway of a tent. The lamp exploded, setting fire to the tent and the dry grass around it.

Mowgli and Gray Brother watched fearfully as the fire raced toward them, moving faster even than Shere Khan, and with a sudden leap, climbed the walls of the cart. Mowgli fell back into the cart, and for a moment could see nothing but black smoke drifting across the stars.

Suddenly the cart surged forward! While being jostled from side to side, Mowgli and Gray Brother looked over the top of the cart and saw the horses running madly. The reins had fallen and Mowgli had no way to stop them or even to steer. The cart was pulled through somebody's clean wash hanging out to dry, and Mowgli had to fight his way from the cool damp grasp of a pair of long johns.

Soon all that he could see of the camp was fire and smoke among the tall trees, and still the horses madly pulled him farther. He smelled the burning water the British used to fill their lamps—kerosene they called it. Fire spun off both wheels, and it climbed closer to the big barrels of kerosene the cart carried. Mowgli knew that when the fire touched the barrels, he and Gray Brother would die, killed in the same kind of explosion that started the fire in the first place.

The cart bounced, and the wheels flew off in bits in all directions, setting the jungle ablaze. The horses, terrified of the fire they themselves were pulling, plunged off the path and pulled the remains of the cart down a hill into the jungle. Mowgli and Gray Brother were thrown about as the cart bumped against roots and stones.

Mowgli saw that he could no longer put off taking his only chance. He held Gray Brother tight against his body and leapt. Very close behind him the kerosene barrels exploded. The last thing Mowgli remembered was the heat and terrible pressure of the explosion on his back.

Moments before, while Mowgli sprawled in the cart with Gray Brother, Major Brydon saw Shere Khan stalking Nathoo, and he took careful aim with his rifle. He squeezed the trigger, but the rifle failed to fire. The major swore at the jammed weapon and threw it down. He saw another rifle a few feet away, leaning against a crate, behind which Buldeo crouched in fear. Before he could get it, the flaming cart shot past the major, spreading a wall of flame between him and the rifle.

"Buldeo!" Brydon cried. "Throw me that rifle."

Buldeo saw that Nathoo was in danger, so instead of throwing the rifle, he smiled and ran off into the jungle.

"Buldeo, you bloody coward!" Major Brydon called after him. But Shere Khan was still stalking Nathoo, slowly backing him into a corner, so there was nothing for Major Brydon to do but gather all his courage. He curled himself up as tightly as he could and rolled through the fire. It was hot and it snapped at him, but he got through all right and grabbed the rifle.

Nearby another tent boomed as it went up in flames.

Brydon lifted the rifle to his cheek and looked through the sight until he found Shere Khan. "I have you now," he said, and was about to squeeze the trigger when a man leapt between the rifle and the tiger with his back to Brydon. Frustrated, Brydon lowered his rifle, then he saw who it was.

"Get back, Nathoo!" Brydon cried.

But even as Brydon cried Shere Khan lashed out at Nathoo with his enormous paw and slashed him as if with knives. The power of the blow threw Nathoo back, nearly to Brydon's feet. Nathoo lay at an unnatural angle. His chest had been torn open, and his face was nearly gone. A doctor was not needed to say that Nathoo was dead.

There was a deadness inside Major Brydon, too, a great surrender to Shere Khan and the alien jungle around him. In India, Nathoo had been the closest thing he'd had to a friend, and now that thing was gone. Brydon was aware that soldiers and guides gathered around him, but he was not yet ready to take notice of them.

The Attack of Shere Khan

A sudden explosion shocked him out of his daze, and he looked up. A fireball rose over the jungle near the ravine they'd crossed that day. It could only have come from the cart carrying Mowgli.

"Where's Mowgli, Father?" Kitty asked.

The major hadn't even been aware that she'd been standing next to him. She was covered with soot, and her arm had been cut, but otherwise, she seemed blessedly whole.

"He's gone, Kat," Major Brydon said as he took her into his arms. "The boy is gone."

❧ 3 ❧

Alone in the Jungle

Mowgli knew he was alive because his arms hurt. His eyes were shut tight, and he was hanging by both hands from a branch. He was sure that if he'd been dead, his arms would not have hurt him so.

He opened his eyes cautiously and wished he had not, for he found that the branch he hung from was wedged under a boulder a long way above the ground. The moon shone on trees that looked like moss below him.

Something squirmed around on his chest and he was afraid that some animal or insect had taken up residence. Then he remembered Gray Brother, and in a moment the cub poked his head out the top of Mowgli's shirt and looked around eagerly.

Above them the branch started to crackle, and a moment later it snapped. Mowgli fell, and for the second time that evening he was certain he'd breathed his last breath. But he fell only ten feet or so before he landed hard on a rocky ledge. How wide the ledge was he did not know, and he did not want to find out the hard way, so he felt along, until he was surprised to feel a large cool wet outcropping— like a doorknob. He opened his eyes and was terrified to find himself staring eye to eye with Shere Khan!

Shere Khan roared at him, showing teeth as long as sabers. Mowgli stumbled back and was soon falling again. He did not fall far before he struck a piece of palm bark the size of a sled. (Mowgli had never seen a sled, of course, but you certainly have.) He held on to both sides of the bark and cried out with excitement as he slid down the mountainside faster and faster. The wind blew at him, and he bumped along, and by first pulling up one side of the bark and then the other he was able to steer around trees, and taken altogether, he would have enjoyed the entire experience if he hadn't worried about Shere Khan above him and the unknown below.

When it seemed that going faster would tear the hair right off his head, the palm bark briefly flew through the air and then settled with a big splash onto a stream that looked like silver in the moonlight.

"Bapu!" Mowgli cried forlornly.

Only an echo answered him.

Gray Brother sat between his legs. Mowgli found small comfort in petting him as they floated downstream on their boat made of bark. The day had been so exhausting and the ride on the stream was so gentle that Mowgli soon fell asleep.

He was awakened by a squirt of water hitting his face. He sat up suddenly and saw with some relief that day had come. He was in a small rocky valley. Sitting around him on the rocks, watching him intently, was a tribe of monkeys. Gray Brother sat nearby, vigorously scratching himself behind the ear with one foot.

"Do you know the way to Major Brydon's camp?" Mowgli asked without much hope.

The monkeys howled and rocked back and forth and laughed and pointed at him.

Stupid monkeys, Mowgli thought.

In the silence that followed the monkeys' outburst, the sounds of the jungle pressed in on Mowgli and frightened him. He heard laughs and roars and growls and trumpets and titters and birdsong of all types. It seemed to him that the jungle had never been so full of noise; as far as Mowgli was concerned, each sound represented an unknown danger.

Then a noise separated itself from the others — it was the howl of a wolf. Gray Brother gave the call an answering squeak and ran into the jungle.

He knew that following Gray Brother would certainly lead to more trouble, but he had promised Nathoo to guard the wolf with his life. Mowgli was not the type who took such promises lightly. As he ran into the jungle after Gray Brother, lightning flashed and slow rain fell in big warm drops. Thunder rolled closer.

"Gray Brother!" Mowgli called as he ran. The thunder seemed like the bellow of another animal, and the lightning like the flashing of its eyes.

Between one lightning flash and another, Mowgli almost ran into an enormous black panther. It was sleek and muscular and looked as if it could devour him in one bite. Mowgli leapt back.

The panther leapt back, too, and snarled.

"Bagheera," Mowgli said. He had never actually expected to meet one. He was stunned by his own terror and found that he could not move.

The panther approached slowly and circled Mowgli, sniffing at him all the while. Mowgli had no idea whether this was common jungle practice or not, but he was frightened the entire time. Still, when the panther started back into the jungle, Mowgli was disappointed. The panther was company of sorts, and seemingly smarter than the monkeys. Where was Gray Brother?

Somewhere near, Shere Khan roared.

The panther looked around, as did Mowgli.

And then, for no reason Mowgli could understand, the panther stepped toward him again, but growling this time. Mowgli ran away, terrified. Rain was falling more heavily now, and both thunder and lightning were nearly continuous.

Suddenly the panther was in front of him, and Mowgli was forced to change direction or be eaten. Again and again the panther leapt into his path, seemingly herding him. At last, tired, wet, confused, and lonely, Mowgli allowed himself to be maneuvered into a low cave. He had no idea why the panther had worked so hard to get him here, but at least he would be dry.

By light that came in through shafts in the ceiling—along with rainwater—Mowgli saw that he might as well have let the panther eat him. Sitting on rock ledges all around were dozens of wolves that snarled and snapped at him. He retreated toward the cave opening.

Gray Brother pounced in from one side and yapped at the gathering pack, but the wolves were not impressed by his arguments. He continued to yap as he and Mowgli backed away together.

"Thank you for your help, Gray Brother," Mowgli said, "but surely they will tear both of us to pieces."

Even as he said this another wolf, this one nearly the same color as Gray Brother, leapt down to face the pack. Mowgli did not know it then, but this was Raksha, Gray Brother's mother. Raksha and the attacking wolves snarled at each other—neither wanting to give ground till honor had been served—and then the members of the pack slunk back to their various perches.

Mowgli did not know what had just happened, but he was very grateful, and he hugged the big gray wolf while Gray Brother danced around. Raksha made a contented noise back in her throat.

4

The Mischief of the Bandar-log

As the dawn was breaking the wolf pack yelled
Once, twice, and again!
Feet in the jungle that leave no mark!
Eyes that can see in the dark—the dark!
Tongue—give tongue to it! Hark! O hark!
Once, twice, and again!
                    —HUNTING SONG OF MOWGLI'S PACK

After Mowgli became a member of the pack he went on many hunting expeditions, not all of them successful. At least one of them was successful in a surprising way.

One time the pack was stalking a deer who was as unsuspecting as a breadfruit before you pick it. Much to the anger of the pack, Mowgli made a telltale sound, and the deer bounded away.

Joyfully, Mowgli raced after it, arms and legs pumping for all they were worth. He did not see the mud puddle until he skidded in it and landed in it face-first. The rest of the pack was still in full cry after the deer while he sat in the puddle shaking the poor gourd of his head to clear it.

Bagheera the panther snarled in disgust at Mowgli's antics, and walked away.

Feeling that he would never get the hang of being a wolf, Mowgli walked by himself through the jungle, head down, face long. He was not watching where he was going. Suddenly a bear paw batted out at him and almost removed that long face of his.

"Baloo," Mowgli said as he looked at the bear, no more than a cub, really. Still, it was bigger than Mowgli himself. The terrible part, the part that Mowgli could not endure, was that one of Baloo's rear legs was caught most brutally in the jaws of a bear trap. Therefore, as frightened as he was, Mowgli crept forward and gripped one jaw of the cruel trap in each hand and pulled with all his strength.

With a sudden bellow, Baloo jerked free and

turned on Mowgli. Mowgli closed his eyes, expecting at any moment to be raked by the claws of the angry bear cub. When nothing happened, he opened his eyes and saw Baloo's face only inches from his. Baloo began to lick Mowgli, making him laugh. He laughed with relief as much as anything else.

Now, O best beloved, we must take many years at a bite, though the stories of Mowgli's growing up in the jungles of India would fill a shelf full of books. Let me say only that he grew straight and strong and handsome. He wore the skin of an animal he'd killed himself, and the bracelet Kitty had given him. He knew the ways of the animals and could move through the jungle like a ghost. Because of his skill and intelligence, Mowgli became leader of his pack.

Mowgli did not clearly remember Kitty or the circumstances under which she had given him the bracelet, but he knew that it was his and that it was important. Wearing it made him feel good, and gave him further distinction over the wild animals, who did not ornament themselves in that way.

For these reasons the monkeys' mischief was particularly infuriating.

It was a lazy day. Mowgli and Bagheera were stretched out full length on a stout branch of a tree, sleeping. Gray Brother slept at the foot of the tree near Baloo, who was busily scooping honey from a beehive and happily stuffing it into his mouth.

Mowgli felt what he thought was an insect at his wrist, but when he tried to brush it away, he found the furry hand of one of the Bandar-log, the Monkey-People! The monkey taunted him with the bracelet. Mowgli reached for it, and the monkey pulled away. Hundreds of monkeys laughed. The tree seemed to be full of them. The monkey with the bracelet ran away, leaping from branch to branch through the high road of the trees. The other monkeys swarmed after him.

Mowgli hit the ground running, Baloo and Gray Brother close behind. Bagheera remained on his branch because the Bandar-log did not interest him. Besides, he had not yet finished his nap.

Mowgli, Baloo, and Gray Brother tore their way through the jungle while they looked up to keep constant watch on the treetops, now crowded with Bandar-log.

The ground suddenly dipped into a valley

Mowgli had never seen before. Though he would have thought it impossible, the jungle in the valley was even greener and thicker than the jungle he was used to. And most tantalizing of all, far off in the thickest part of the thick jungle he saw the tall thin spires of what was certainly a city!

Mowgli heard the laughter of the Bandar-log. He ran down the hill, and with the help of Baloo and Gray Brother bullied his way through the forest. Soon Baloo and Gray Brother were ready to let the monkeys have the bracelet, but the laughter of the Bandar-log urged Mowgli on. His friends could not abandon him, so they continued to follow.

After what seemed to be a long time, the jungle suddenly stopped at the edge of a great stone courtyard. Yet even here the jungle had invaded, lifting stones with roots, twisting vines around the weathered remains of statues and through windows, so that figs now looked out instead of people.

In the center of the courtyard was a stone statue of a monkey. It was bigger than three elephants and wound about with creepers. The face of the statue was sublimely pleased with itself; it had an enormous mouth, perpetually open, that was obviously the entrance to the massive building that spread for acres around either side of the monkey statue.

An orangutan stepped out onto the lower lip of the statue. He wore oddly matched pieces of clothing and a hat that sparkled in the sunlight with more-than-Oriental splendor. Mowgli had never seen such a thing. It was beautiful, but surely too awkward and heavy to be of any great use.

Mowgli decided that this must be Looey, king of the Bandar-log. But what interested him more than the name and station of this monkey was the fact that he held out the bracelet for Mowgli to see. The monkey made a rude noise with his lips and waddled back into the statue.

Mowgli growled and ran foward. While Baloo and Gray Brother counciled against it, he desperately climbed the statue to the open mouth and pulled himself inside.

He ran through a dark tunnel, brushing spiderwebs from his face, and at last emerged again into the sunlight. He stood at one side of a plaza, facing a building bigger than any he had ever seen. He did not know it was a palace, but it was—built for the pleasure of some young king centuries before. It was brown and green with age, and broken in many places where the jungle had intruded. The walls were painted with pictures of the grand people who had once lived in the city. And though the pictures were terribly weathered, Mowgli could still see that the inhabitants had thought a great deal of themselves. Monkeys were everywhere, lounging, eating, playing, trying to strike the poses of the people in the paintings. The noise and smell were horrendous.

But Mowgli was most interested in King Looey, who stood next to a well on the other side of the plaza waving the bracelet. As Mowgli ran toward him, giving his fearsome battle cry, King Looey stepped over the edge of the well dropped out of sight. Without thinking, Mowgli leapt into the well after him.

He fell for a long time. He had not known digging a hole so deep was possible. Would he come out among the roots of the earth itself? He landed with a splash in a river that had smooth stone sides. He swam across and stood at the edge of the most amazing room he'd ever seen. Light and air came in through ingenious openings in the walls and ceiling. There were piles of gold and silver coins; immense jewel-encrusted elephant howdahs; gold and silver images of forgotten gods; helmets, crested and beaded with pigeon's blood rubies; weapons with diamond encrusted hilts; and jewelry enough to satisfy an entire army of queens. Skeletons were everywhere, some with swords or daggers between their ribs. The walls showed the people of the city in victorious battle.

Mowgli picked up a coin and bit it. It was cold and hard and its taste made his teeth hurt. What was all this useless stuff, and why would men kill each other over it? He picked up a dagger that had a picture of monkeys and a python formed into the hilt from jewels. He immediately cut his finger on the blade. He was surprised that anything could be so sharp. Such a weapon seemed more useful than the other hard things that lay around here, and would help make up for his lack of claws and razor teeth—a lack he had long felt.

Monkeys gathered in windows and doorways and chittered down at him, giving Mowgli the sense that they were waiting for something to happen, though he could not imagine what.

At the far end of the room was a golden statue

of an elephant, as enormous and pleased with itself as the statue of the monkey outside. King Looey stepped out onto the head of the elephant statue and waved the bracelet at him again. Mowgli refused to be led any farther until he knew what King Looey's game was.

Suddenly all the monkeys went quiet, chilling Mowgli as all their laughing and chittering had not.

A python twice as thick as his wrist rose before Mowgli out of a mountain of coins. He was so surprised and frightened that he stumbled back and dropped his dagger. The python weaved up and back. Mowgli shook off the hypnotic movement and grabbed the snake just behind its head. The snake struggled, pushing Mowgli back into the moat. The monkeys howled.

The water foamed with their fight. The python held Mowgli underwater, but he managed to wriggle free. He climbed frantically back to the bank and managed to grab his dagger before the python dragged him back into the water. The python tightened his hold on Mowgli's chest, forcing all the air out of him. He plunged the dagger into the python once, again, and again. At last Mowgli felt the python's grip loosen, and he kicked against the bottom of the moat. He shot to the surface and took a great lungful of air. A moment later he climbed back onto the bank, but on the side away from the hard things. He had had quite enough of them for now and for always—except for the dagger. The dagger had shown its usefulness. Only the python's head showed above water as it swam away.

All around him monkeys applauded and howled and stamped their feet and did somersaults. Looey was leading the applause. Then he threw the bracelet to Mowgli and applauded some more. Mowgli held the bracelet aloft for a moment, feeling his victory rush through his veins like fire. But he soon tired of the admiration of the Bandar-log. He had what he'd come for, and now he could leave.

The monkey people chittered at him as he crossed the plaza, but none dared approach him. They did not chose to challenge he who had defeated Kaa the python.

Mowgli rejoined Baloo and Gray Brother, who were still waiting for him outside the big monkey statue. Gray Brother trotted beside Mowgli, who sliced the dagger through the air as he rode Baloo home in triumph.

They had not quite reached the tree where they'd left Bagheera when something flashed in Mowgli's eyes. He did not know what made the flashing, but he did know that it was nothing that belonged in the jungle.

"That way, Baloo," he said, and pointed with his dagger toward the strange bright light that came and went.

❧ 5 ❧

Waingara Palace

The light that so fascinated Mowgli was reflected off the barrel of the rifle of a British soldier, who—in a relaxed and unambitious way—was guarding a group of officers and ladies who were playing croquet on an improvised field at the side of a broad river. Upstream a ways a waterfall thundered and threw rainbows into the hot still air.

Nearby, Dr. Plumford was teaching a group of young ladies to paint pictures of the local plants and animals. Plumford was an older man in a white suit and pith helmet. While he tried to take himself seriously, he could not quite manage it. The world was a place of marvels, and he knew that he was just one more.

Mowgli did not know any of this when he came down to the other side of the river. He only watched with amazement the people in strange clothes, doing things he had never imagined, for reasons he did not understand.

The man in the white suit—whom we know to be Dr. Plumford—led his girls along a path that came near a bamboo bridge over the river.

"This bridge," Plumford said gravely, "separates mankind from the animal kingdom." He pointed to a weather-beaten sign plunged into the hard earth. It was written in Hindi. "This sign says, 'Beware! Cross this bridge at your own peril. He who enters the jungle will look death in the face.'" He read the sign dramatically, as if he were reciting for the stage.

"Actually, Doctor," one of the young women said as she stepped forward, smiling, "the sign says, 'Beware! This bridge is old.'" From Mowgli's viewpoint, she was the most beautiful of the group, which would have been bewildering enough to a boy who did not often see humans of any kind—but was even more bewildering because there was something familiar about her.

The other girls laughed, and even Plumford smiled. "All right, ladies," he said. "I suppose I exaggerated a bit. Come along," he said as he led them farther along the path, "we'll do our painting down here."

The group walked on, all except for the beautiful one and three of her friends. They giggled over the idea of danger lurking on the other side of the bamboo bridge, which, truth to tell, except for the croquet, looked very much like the side of the bridge they were on. Still, it did get dark very quickly under the trees. Alice dared Rose to cross the bridge. Rose would not, and Margaret agreed with her. But the most beautiful of them set down her painting things. "I will," she said. And before her friends could protest, she ran across the bridge.

Mowgli watched her breathlessly.

While Mowgli watched the beautiful woman tentatively explore his side of the river, a dashing cavalry officer rode up to the croquet players. The officer was Captain William Boone. He was in the company of Tabaqui, a very unsavory-looking man who, despite the heat, was dressed all in fur.

Waingara Palace

"About time, Billy boy," one of the croquet-playing officers cried as Boone leapt from his horse. This was Lieutenant Charles Wilkins, a man who was once described as being barbered within an inch of his life. Everything about him was sharp and neat. "Bugger!" Wilkins cried as he slapped the back of his neck. "I don't know which I hate more, this country or the things that live in it."

Boone laughed. "Don't bite the hand that feeds you, Charles. We came to this country to make our fortunes, remember?"

Boone spotted Alice and Rose and Margaret painting down by the river, and he went to greet them, hoping that the beautiful one was somewhere about. He was surprised to see the hem of her dress as it swished into the jungle on the far side of the river. He frowned and followed.

The beautiful one was in the jungle picking red flowers. She had never before seen any so large or fragrant, and here was a whole jungle full of them. She heard a growl and stopped, suddenly fearing that Dr. Plumford had been right about how much danger really prowled on this side of the river. She turned to walk back the way she had come when another growl came from even closer, then another.

She ran and at a turn in the path was confronted by the strangest young man she'd ever seen. He was undeniably handsome, and he fairly rippled with muscles under his tanned skin. His dark hair was long and shaggy, as if it had never been cut.

"Stay back," she warned.

Mowgli held out a red flower. He'd done this before, long ago. He remembered the name Kitty. Could this be Kitty? She had grown so!

Slowly, hands trembling, she took the flower and he leaned in for his kiss. Surprising both of them, she punched him in the jaw.

Before Mowgli could do more than rub his injury, Baloo lumbered out of the jungle and growled a greeting. Kitty seemed to be terribly frightened by this, though Mowgli could not imagine why. It was just Baloo—silly old bear.

Then Mowgli, as unsophisticated in the ways of humans as he was, realized that this was his opportunity to impress Kitty with his fighting skill. He stooped into a fighting crouch and circled Baloo, who seemed confused by the turn of events. Then Mowgli rushed Baloo, and they wrestled as they often did. He was having such a good time that it was a few minutes before Mowgli thought to check on what Kitty thought of his bravery. He was very disappointed to see that she was gone.

Boone caught up with Kitty as she was rushing out of the jungle. She rushed right into him.

"Whoa, my Kitty girl," he said. "No one's supposed to cross the bridge, you know. It's dangerous." He leaned in to kiss her, as Mowgli had done earlier. Kitty didn't punch him, but she did dance a step out of his grasp. "Not in public, Billy," she cautioned.

"What public?" he asked. "We're surrounded by jungle!" He reached for her again, but missed as Kitty walked toward the bridge. "What's the matter with this side of the bridge?" he asked, grinning. "Afraid the savage in me may come out?" He growled playfully at her.

Kitty turned to smile at him. He really was *most* charming. Boone took this opportunity to swing her up into his arms. Faster than thought, Mowgli leapt from the jungle and tore Kitty free of Boone. He placed himself between Kitty and Boone, snarling and ready for a fight.

Boone quickly recovered from his surprise. "Touch what belongs to me, you bloody savage, and by sunset I'll mount your head on my wall!"

"It's all right, William. He thought you were attacking me."

"Cheeky little . . ." Boone held up his fists, British bare-knuckle boxing style.

"Billy, please," Kitty cried. "You'll hurt him."

"Quite likely," Boone said with pleasure.

But when Boone jabbed at him, Mowgli grabbed his fist. Boone was stunned for only a moment before he jabbed with his other fist. Mowgli grabbed that, too, and pushed Boone into the river.

By this time the croquet party was crossing the bridge. Boone was angry, aware that he had been made a fool of by this savage. It relieved him only a little that the jungle lad managed to throw a number of other officers as well into the river. Not even Wilkins, who swung a branch like a club, could make any headway against him.

Mowgli thought he was safe, so he picked up the red flower and was about to hand it to Kitty when he saw the horror on her face. He turned, but was too late to avoid Tabaqui, who hit him hard with a rock. He was about to strike Mowgli again when Bagheera and Baloo leapt out of the jungle snarling and bellowing.

The British retreated across the bridge, the women shrieking, the men cursing, none staying for the fight. By the time they had evened the odds with rifles and were ready to return, Mowgli, Bagheera, and Baloo were gone.

Baloo took Mowgli to a hilltop, where he and Bagheera hoped the fresh wind would revive him, and after a while it did. But Mowgli continued to sit and turn a red flower in his hands, and to watch the fires of a village many miles away. Gray Brother came to sit, too. Mowgli acknowledged his arrival, then went back to his thinking.

As daylight shone like a forge just below the horizon, Mowgli suddenly leapt up, scratched behind the ears of each of his friends, and ran down the hill. Gray Brother barked at Bagheera and Baloo, then ran after him.

Mowgli ran through the jungle with Gray Brother loping beside him, and at last they came to Waingara, a village of man. He told Gray Brother to stay behind, then he dropped out of a tree onto a rooftop. From there, he observed the market square, where to show their holiness, men charmed snakes, climbed ropes attached only at the bottom, walked across hot coals, and swallowed swords or fire. Other men, less holy but more practical, hawked foodstuffs of various types. Women jabbered at the well. Children ran everywhere, getting into everything. It was the intersection of madness and commerce.

Mowgli did not allow the market square to distract him for long. He sniffed the air, got the scent, then ran across roofs and down alleys, toward the palace just beyond the village.

Waingara Palace was not as magnificent as the palace the Bandar-log inhabited, but it was much newer. Everything worked, and it kept the jungle out, but it could not keep Mowgli out. Grabbing cracks he could barely see, he climbed the outside wall. He called to a flock of doves that lived on the wall's decorative moldings, and they flew up as one, distracting a sentry long enough to allow Mowgli to leap over the wall and onto a parapet that was long and wide enough to be a street.

He ran down the street, rounded a corner, and saw a line of elephants sedately approaching a line of camels. To follow the scent, Mowgli needed to cross this street. He called to the elephants, insulting them. The elephants bellowed, frightening the camels, and soon the lines of animals were tangled, with noisy rearing beasts everywhere.

Mowgli clung to the cinches holding the howdah to one of the elephants, and it carried him through the confusion to a doorway. He leapt off, allowing the elephant to continue its rampage. Mowgli ran up a flight of stairs and was surprised to run into Lieutenant Wilkins. Wilkins swore as he pulled his pistol from his holster. Mowgli ran, still following the magic scent.

"Sound the alarm!" Wilkins cried. "Intruder alert! Intruder alert!"

While shots were fired, whistles blew, and men began to run below, Mowgli found his way to the room of his dreams. The noises did not bother him. He was not much concerned with the affairs of men.

When he was in the middle of the room, Kitty turned away from her balcony and saw him. "I must say, you are persistent. But you must go or they'll catch you."

Of course, Mowgli could not understand a word she was saying. He only handed her the red flower he'd brought with him and leaned in for his kiss, hoping to fare better this time.

"What is it with you and flowers and kissing?" she asked as she pushed him away, but gently.

Mowgli took heart in the fact that she did not hit him, and he began to explore the room. There was a thing that looked like the red flower but was very hot, and bit him when he touched it. Another thing was white and cool and looked a little like cream, but tasted terrible. He could not endure seeing animals in cages, so he freed a parrot Kitty was keeping as a pet. All the while Kitty kept asking him to do something and pulling him toward a doorway.

"Can you speak anything?" Kitty asked. "English? Hindi? Anything?"

The noise from below got louder, causing Mowgli to wonder if perhaps he ought to leave before it arrived.

"I am Kitty Brydon," she said as she pointed to herself. "Do you have a name?"

Mowgli recognized the word Kitty. He knew it was a name.

"Mowgli," he said as he thumped his chest.

Kitty seemed astonished. "That's not possible," she said.

Then Mowgli slid off the bracelet the earlier Kitty had given him a long time ago, and gave it to the Kitty who stood before him. She looked in astonishment from the bracelet to him.

"Mowgli?" she asked as her eyes got wide.

They were staring at each other over an abyss of time and experience when the door burst open, allowing Boone and Wilkins to run into the room. Boone leveled his pistol at Mowgli.

"You're mine now, you bloody savage," he said.

🐍 6 🐍

Dungeon Charity

"No!" Kitty cried, and pushed Boone's hand aside just as he fired.

Boone's shot nicked Mowgli in the arm, and the wound hurt more than anything he had ever felt. He backed off, and for a moment and glared at Boone with a hatred entirely unfamiliar to him—jungle hunters are often hungry, but they rarely hate.

Before Boone had a chance to fire again, Mowgli ran for the balcony and jumped. He fell straight down two stories—landed the way Bagheera had taught him, on his feet—avoided the shots of a sentry, and fell again.

When he was back at ground level, he raced for

the market square, where he knew he could confuse and perhaps escape those who were chasing him. He tipped over carts of fruit and scattered rugs, pots, and jugs. People screamed and shook their fists and chased him. The crowd of villagers got in the way of the soldiers that poured from the palace.

Mowgli leapt for a rope being made to stand up straight in the air by one of the holy men. Mowgli climbed higher and higher, to the surprised outrage of the protesting holy man near the top. He climbed *over* the holy man and jumped across onto a roof.

He did not understand why the soldiers wanted to hurt him. He'd only come to visit Kitty. Tears filled his eyes as he made his way from roof to roof and at last dropped into an empty back alley that smelled like the worst of the Bandar-log's palace. The noise and shooting were far away. Perhaps he would now have a chance to study his present situation.

He ran down the alley looking for the outside wall of the village, and rounded a corner to confront another face from his past—an unshaven face with jagged teeth and an unfriendly leer. While Mowgli gaped, the man who owned the face struck him in the head with the butt of a rifle. The world went red, and then black.

"Good work, Buldeo," Captain Boone said as he and Wilkins approached. Boone turned Mowgli over with one foot and saw Mowgli's jeweled dagger. The emblem of monkeys and a python on the hilt was most curious.

Buldeo reached for it and stared at it greedily.

"Queen's evidence," Boone said as he snatched the dagger away from Buldeo.

"Maybe," Buldeo said as he mounted a white horse being held by his friend Tabaqui, who was also mounted. "But it has many brothers." He and Tabaqui rode away as the villagers arrived in a rush, yelling and reaching for Mowgli.

"Brothers, eh?" Boone said. He and Wilkins pushed the villagers aside and roughly dragged Mowgli away.

Know you, O best beloved, that there was a witness to all that had happened in the alley. Gray Brother watched from a wall. He understood neither what had been said nor why it had been said, but he could see that Mowgli needed help. Gray Brother leapt from the wall, back into the jungle, and loped away.

Mowgli was vaguely aware of being hauled none too gently back to Waingara Palace, then down into dark damp smelly places where he had not been before. Rats called to him and asked if he'd brought any food. He was taken past a fire that smoldered orange in a big box, and pushed down onto a chair. An enormous soldier who reminded Mowgli of King Looey stepped up to him, slapping a thing like a table leg in his hand. Mowgli was aware that he'd come to a bad place, and even that his sad state was somehow Boone's fault, but he still failed to understand *why*.

"Ah, Captain Boone and Lieutenant Wilkins, me favorite officers," the big man said. He saluted with the table leg. "What do we 'ave 'ere, then?"

"Sergeant Harley, this savage tried to kill Colonel Brydon's daughter," Boone said.

"You don't say?" Harley remarked, only moderately interested. He suddenly grabbed Mowgli by the hair and yanked his head back. "We can't be 'avin' any o' that, can we, my chick?"

Though friends in the jungle could play rough, such play was always roughhousing among equals. Harley was clearly not playing, and yet Mowgli supposed that Harley would not eat him. What, then, was this all about? Mowgli could smell the man's foul breath. He could not imagine what Harley had been eating. Mowgli snapped at him and Harley let go of his hair.

"I'll enjoy working on this one, I will," Harley said as he smiled.

"We found this on him," Wilkins said.

Harley's eyes widened when he saw the dagger. He grabbed Mowgli's hair again and shook it, making colors explode before Mowgli's eyes. "Listen up, me little brown friend. Tell Uncle 'Arley where you got that dagger." When Mowgli said nothing, Harley struck him on the shoulder with the table leg. Mowgli cried out and kicked Harley between the legs.

"Oof!" Harley said, and curled over in pain, a look of surprise on his face. He recovered enough to strike Mowgli again and again with his table leg. Mowgli leapt to his feet and backed away from Harley, his arms raised for protection.

"Sergeant Harley!" someone called out.

Immediately, the beating stopped. Mowgli did not know why, but he was grateful. When he saw the man who had given the order, Mowgli once again had the feeling that he'd known him before in another life. This realization added to his confusion. He did not know that the man was your grandfather himself—Colonel Brydon, Kitty's father.

No one saw Boone slip Mowgli's dagger into his tunic.

"Come to order, please," Colonel Brydon called as he stepped farther into the room. Boone, Wilkins, and Harley snapped to attention.

"This is the intruder, sir," Boone said.

"I am aware of that," Brydon said, "but it is not necessary to beat a prisoner to detain him."

"I was about to suggest the same thing to Sergeant Harley myself, sir," Boone said.

"Well then?" Brydon asked.

" 'E kicked me, sir," Harley explained, kind of whining.

"Kicked you, eh, Sergeant?" Brydon said, trying to suppress a smile. "What's his name?"

"We don't know, sir," Wilkins said.

Boone stood a little stiffer. "But I can assure the colonel that I take very personally the savage's intrusion into his daughter's private quarters."

Colonel Brydon looked at Mowgli and smiled warmly. He spoke words that Mowgli did not understand, but they sounded friendly. He would have answered if he could. "Hmm," Brydon said, and studied Mowgli

"Hasn't said a word yet, sir," Boone said.

Brydon walked back to the stairs, then turned. "Very well, Boone. You're a good man, and I'll entrust him to your care. And you, Sergeant," Brydon went on sternly while he shook a finger in Harley's direction, "I'm sure I don't have remind you that our mission in this country is to bring justice and enlightenment. We are proper and civilized. We are not savages. So show the boy a little charity." He climbed the stairs again. "Carry on," he said.

Boone, Wilkins, and Harley watched Mowgli. Mowgli watched them right back, which they seemed to find amusing.

"I'll give you charity," Harley said when Brydon was gone. "It'll be a fine serving o' bare knuckles for you, my chick."

Outside, a wolf howled, then another, then another. Soon the night was full of music. The three British soldiers looked around worriedly. Mowgli smiled and raced into a cell where a barred window looked out onto the courtyard of the palace. He lifted his head to howl in answer, but was stopped by Harley, who pulled him away from the window and shoved him into a corner full of ancient damp straw and many tiny creatures. Mowgli lifted his head again to answer the wolf call, and Harley slapped him hard.

"We'll have none o' that, my chick." Harley went out and slammed the door shut with a clang. "None o' that," he said again, and pointed the table leg at him through the bars. He glanced at Boone and Wilkins, then looked in the direction of the window. Boone and Wilkins seemed a little nervous, too.

Mowgli took what comfort he could in the company of the tiny brothers with whom he shared his cell, and in listening to the gathering of the wolves.

7

Kitty's Project

The next morning Colonel Brydon was surprised to be visited in his office by his daughter. She seemed very serious and determined.

"Father, what are you doing with that boy?"

Brydon supposed that pretending ignorance would get him nowhere. "More to the point, my dear," he said gently, "what was that boy doing in your quarters?"

"He's gentle and harmless," Kitty protested.

"Tell that to Sergeant Harley," Brydon said, chuckling.

"Excuse me?"

"Nothing. That boy is Captain Boone's concern

now. And speaking of Captain Boone, any news for your old father?"

"Please, Father," Kitty said as she waved all that aside, "we have more important matters to—"

Dr. Plumford bustled in, already in midconversation. "Isn't it all so very exciting?" he asked as if everybody knew exactly what he was talking about.

"What? What's exciting?" Brydon asked. He did not enjoy days when his visitors were two conversational steps ahead of him.

Kitty and Dr. Plumford traded glances. Apparently, the colonel's visitors were further ahead of him than he'd imagined.

"Father, that boy—he's Mowgli."

"Mowgli?" Brydon asked, surprised. "You mean poor old Nathoo's son? The boy who . . . ?" Brydon was upset by the suggestion. For one thing, it seemed so unlikely. For another, it would somehow complicate the situation enormously. "It can't be," he said. "No five-year-old child could survive in the jungle for ten minutes, let alone for fifteen years."

"He wouldn't be five anymore," Plumford reminded him.

Kitty said nothing, but held up the bracelet Mowgli had given to her only a few hours before. She set it on her father's desk and waited.

Brydon picked up the bracelet and stared at it in disbelief. "This was your mother's bracelet. I gave it to you when—"

"Yes, and I gave it to a little boy named Mowgli. You remember. You were furious with me." Kitty seemed to take some pleasure at the memory.

Brydon stood up and turned to the window, though he was too engrossed in his own thoughts to see the courtyard below. He had liked old Nathoo, and so felt some responsibility to his son, just as the British had some responsibility to India. As a matter of fact, this business with Mowgli was exactly the British and Indian situation in miniature.

"It is our duty to help him," Kitty insisted.

"Could be an interesting case study," Plumford said as he leaned forward earnestly. "Chart his development, you know, his ability to reason. Find out what being raised by animals is like."

Brydon turned away from the window and cocked an eyebrow in their direction. "You two have thought this all through, haven't you?"

Kitty smiled shyly and made a circle on the carpet with one toe.

"We've prepared a place for him," Plumford admitted. "In the garden shed. Outside."

"So he won't feel so confined," Kitty added.

Actually, Brydon was pleased that Kitty and Plumford had come to him with this scheme. A dungeon was really no place for a boy, and who knew what Harley might do to him when nobody was around? "Very well," he said.

"Splendid," Plumford exclaimed, and rubbed his hands together with eagerness.

Mowgli had never been so miserable. The three men—the two thin ones and the one who looked like King Looey—kept asking him questions and hitting him with things. Sometimes one of them shook the dagger in his face, but he'd already seen it, so even that made no sense.

"He's an animal," Harley said as he ripped apart a chicken with his hands and stuffed the meat into his mouth. Grease had already congealed on his beard. "A real animal," he insisted.

Boone and Wilkins shook their heads in disgust. Then Boone walked over to Mowgli's cell. "Now then, my good man," he said pleasantly, "how about a word for me?"

Mowgli growled warningly, and Boone stepped back. He had never before heard a man make a noise so much like that of a tiger.

Mowgli looked up, having caught the magic scent. A moment later Kitty came down the steps, lifting her skirts a little to keep them out of the muck. Boone, Wilkins, and Harley stared at her, astonished, as she greeted them.

"Katherine," Boone said, "this area is off limits to civilians, and it is certainly no place for a lady."

"Then it's a good job I am neither a civilian nor a lady. I am, however, here on official business. Dr. Plumford and I have discovered that your new prisoner is the jungle boy the villagers all talk about."

"The one raised by animals?" Wilkins asked.

"Indeed," Kitty said. "We want to teach him to speak, civilize him, help him reenter society. If"—she looked with innocent directness at Boone—"I can get *your* permission, Captain Boone."

"He's vicious and uncivilized," Boone warned.

Kitty saw Mowgli for the first time. He had been standing in shadow at the back of the cell, and so she can be forgiven for not seeing him earlier. "Good Lord," she said as she rushed forward, "what did you do to him?"

Boone affected a sad spiritual expression on his face. "We tried to stop him from hurting himself," he said.

"But he's a bit mad, I'm afraid," Wilkins went on.

"Done it to 'imself, 'e 'as, miss," Harley said with a vigorous nod.

Kitty frowned. They were not describing the Mowgli she knew, not even the one who had visited her in her quarters. She put out her hand.

"Watch your fingers, miss," Harley cautioned. " 'E'll bite 'em off."

Mowgli stepped forward and Boone and Wilkins pulled their pistols. Kitty knew they were being silly. She touched Mowgli's hand.

"Kitty," he said as he smiled.

"Mowgli," Kitty said, and returned the smile.

While Mowgli and Kitty held a conversation that consisted mostly of smiles and the repetition of their names, Boone pulled Wilkins aside. "If he can be taught to speak," Boone whispered, "he can be made to talk."

Wilkins nodded.

Kitty, Dr. Plumford, and a trusted native butler attempted to civilize Mowgli. Teaching him to bathe was a trial, and teaching him to use dining utensils was even worse. Generally, Dr. Plumford ended a lesson only after he was thoroughly soaked, or covered with mashed potatoes.

The three teachers took Mowgli to a tailor in the marketplace and had him fitted for a full wardrobe of suits. The clothes itched, and he couldn't move properly, but Mowgli wore them anyway because he could see that wearing them made Kitty look at him with new appreciation.

The tailor's shop was built into the outer wall of Waingara village, and while he was in the changing room Mowgli saw Baloo and Gray Brother looking in at him with amusement and confusion. Mowgli tried to get them to leave before somebody saw them, but they refused to go. He posed for them in his new clothes, but they only grunted and shook their heads.

The teachers' major success was in teaching Mowgli to speak recognizable English, and when he managed to tell Kitty he thought she was beautiful, it pleased them both.

Kitty's friends were intrigued by Mowgli the way they might be intrigued by an exotic animal. "Is he so very wild?" Alice asked as she, Kitty, Margaret, and Rose took the air on a palace street one day.

"Utterly savage," Kitty said, exaggerating only a little.

"Aren't you afraid of him?" Margaret asked.

"Sometimes," Kitty admitted.

"How did he survive all those years in the jungle?" Alice asked.

"He was very cunning," Kitty said, enjoying her chance to explain. "He learned to kill with his own two hands. Like that!" She snapped her fingers, causing her friends to jump. "Then he'd eat his prey raw." For effect, she lifted her hands to her mouth and pantomimed eating with loud grunts. She had no idea if she had described anything near the truth, but her friends were satisfactorily disgusted.

"How does Captain Boone feel about your spending so much time with another man?" Rose asked after they had recovered from Kitty's flamboyant description.

"You do spend an awful lot of time with him," Alice agreed.

Kitty dared not look at them. "I'm Mowgli's teacher," she said. "That is all."

"Very well," Margaret said.

"Captain Boone is the most handsome, dashing officer in all of India," Kitty said, "and we"— she smiled—"and we are the perfect couple." She was about to follow her friends into a stall where fine silver was sold when someone grabbed her by the arm and pulled her to one side. She had her mouth open to cry out when she saw that her abductor was Mowgli.

"What are you doing?" Kitty asked, still a little flustered.

"I take you to my friends. Make *intra-dumtions.*"

"*Intro-ductions.*"

"Yes, those," Mowgli said, and smiled. "You come. See my home." He put out his hand to her.

Kitty hesitated for just a moment, then took it.

Mowgli led Kitty farther into the jungle than she had ever gone, or ever imagined going. Yet, because Mowgli was so confident of what to do, of where to go, Kitty was not afraid. She was only fascinated.

Mowgli carried her up a tree, and they swung on a vine from that one to another. It was exhilarating, enchanting. Mowgli's touch was strong and sure. They slid down a vine to a beautiful lake. Nothing moved on it, and it seemed less like a lake than like a piece of sky that had fallen faceup on the jungle floor.

"Let us be swimming," Mowgli said as he pulled off his shirt and started on his trowsers.

"What?" Kitty asked, astonished. "With our clothes off?"

"Does man swim with his clothes on, then?"

Kitty glanced around. "What if someone should see us?" she asked.

"Who?"

Kitty had to admit that they were miles from anything resembling civilization, with dense jungle in between. Excited by her own boldness, Kitty started to remove her dress. She stopped, suddenly frightened when a gray wolf and a big black bear wandered out of the jungle. She hid behind Mowgli.

"Animools are friends," Mowgli said as he led Kitty to Gray Brother. Her hand was trembling when he laid it gently on the wolf's head. His fur was surprisingly soft.

Then Mowgli ran to Baloo and hugged him. It was the most satisfying thing he'd done in weeks. Baloo bellowed with delight.

"Baloo, my best friend," Mowgli said.

"Isn't that the same animal you saved me from that first day by the bridge?" Kitty asked.

Mowgli smiled shyly and shrugged. What else could he do?

In any case, the mood was broken, and a swim without clothes seemed out of the question. Instead, Mowgli led Kitty along the stream that fed the lake. They walked hand in hand while Baloo and Gray Brother followed. The day was magic.

"Can you talk with the animals?" Kitty asked. Such a question would have seemed ridiculous only hours before, but she felt as if she were in a dream where such questions made as much sense as a dictionary.

"Yes, but it is not the talk of men," Mowgli said as he lifted a baby monkey from a low branch. "You see," he went on, "with animals, every move and sound has meaning." He handed the monkey to Kitty and she was delighted. It sat

on her arm with its tail wrapped around her
wrist. Possibly because of Mowgli's presence, it
seemed entirely without fear.

"The jungle has many tongues," Mowgli said,
"and I speak them all."

They walked more, and soon the monkey
leapt away on business of its own.

"If you could have spoken to me that first
time we met," Kitty said, "what would you have
said? What did you feel?"

"Fire," Mowgli said.

"Fire?"

"A great fire," he said, and smiled as men have
smiled at women since the beginning. He
touched his heart. They stopped and Kitty
turned to look into his eyes. Was this animal
magnetism, the strange attraction she felt for
him? She could look into his eyes forever. He
leaned in for a kiss, and she pulled away, suddenly frightened—not of him, but of herself, of
her intense feelings.

"It's late," she said. She was still shaking with
the effort of turning away from Mowgli. "We'd
better go. Captain Boone is expecting me." She
walked toward the jungle, though she had no
idea in which direction Waingara Palace lay.

He walked after her and took her hand, pulled her back toward the stream. "No," he said. "Please stay here with me."

"I can't," Kitty said, confused. "There are conventions, formalities, things that are just not done." Like setting up housekeeping with a wild boy in the middle of the jungle, she thought.

"I don't understand."

Kitty could not meet his eyes. "I must do what's right," she said as much to herself as to him. "I must do what's proper. I must do what's civilized."

"What must *I* do?" Mowgli asked.

Suddenly Kitty saw it all, the entire grand plan. "We must make *you* proper and civilized as well, so that I—" She cut herself off, embarrassed. "So that *any* British girl would be honored to have you as her escort."

"I want to be civilized," Mowgli said, though the only part of civilization he liked so far was Kitty Brydon.

He took her back to Waingara Palace and applied himself to his studies, hoping that one day she would be honored to have him as her escort. Weeks passed, during which Mowgli learned to waltz, and what to say if he met any of

Young Mowgli with his newfound
friend Gray Brother.

An older Mowgli (Jason Scott Lee) with his good friend Gray Brother in the jungle.

◆ Mowgli standing proud in front of the Lost City of Hanuman— Monkey City. ◆

◆ The self-assured Captain Boone (Cary Elwes). ◆

❧ The beautiful Kitty (Lena Headey) watches the ball around her, perhaps awaiting her love. ☙

☙ The elegant Kitty looks to Captain Boone, her beau. ❧

☙ Kitty and Doctor Plumford (John Cleese) trying to teach Mowgli the English ways. ❧

☙ The now-westernized Mowgli looking uncomfortable in his European clothes. ❧

Mowgli introduces his friend Bagheera to Kitty.

Doctor Plumford and Baloo get acquainted.

🖎 Boone trying to protect himself as he uses
Kitty as his hostage. 🖎

☙ Surrounded by the wolf pack, Kitty and Mowgli finally share an intimate moment. ❧

Kitty's Project

Kitty's friends in the market square, and about the outside world through pictures in books. He took some of his training back to the jungle, but when he tried to kiss Baloo on the paw, the bear batted Mowgli to the ground.

During these weeks, Captain Boone was also busy. His jealousy of Mowgli grew day by day, but he did nothing about it because he needed Mowgli. The savage would soon take him to the place where he had gotten the dagger. After that, Kitty would be his again.

Then one night near sunset, O best beloved, Kitty and Mowgli stood on a parapet overlooking the palace and the jungle beyond. She kissed him, thanking him for a wonderful day. When she ran off, Mowgli was left a little dazed.

Boone and Wilkins were idling below, and they both saw what Kitty had done.

"Was that a kiss I saw?" Wilkins teased. "Seems you have competition, old boy."

Boone angrily grabbed Wilkins by the throat and pushed him hard against the railing.

"I was joking," Wilkins managed to squeak out. "Joking."

Boone held Wilkins that way for a moment, then let him go and helped him straighten his

71

tunic. All the anger seemed to have gone out of him. He looked over the parapet at the jungle, calm as the air.

"She's the colonel's daughter," Boone said. "She serves a purpose."

"You *are* ambitious," Wilkins remarked, careful to make it an admiring remark.

While Boone and Wilkins discussed the colonel's daughter, and Mowgli stood on his parapet watching the sun go down and remembering *exactly* what Kitty's kiss felt like, Kitty herself quietly entered the quarters she shared with her father. She knew she had promised to be back hours before, and she was a mess from waltzing in the jungle—her hair down around her shoulders, her skirts peppered with dead leaves, her shoes muddy.

"Katherine," her father called as she stepped lightly across the foyer. She backed up and stood at his office doorway, her hands behind her back. He marched toward her looking very angry.

"Hello, Father," Kitty said, hoping for the best.

"Is that all you have to say? Hello, Father? I've had men combing the whole bloody district for you! You were with the jungle boy, weren't you?"

"His name is Mowgli, Father," Kitty said firmly.

"He's a savage," Colonel Brydon insisted as he paced up and down between his desk and his daughter. "Raised by animals, and bred in the jungle. It's not right for a girl of your standing, of your—well, people are starting to talk."

"People always talk."

"It's not done, do you hear me?" Colonel Brydon cried as he shook a finger at Kitty. "It is just not done."

"What's not done?" Kitty asked, pretending exasperation. She knew exactly what her father was talking about. Her thoughts about Mowgli had not always been the thoughts of a teacher for a student. What she did not know was how her father had guessed. "I haven't done anything!" she went on.

Colonel Brydon harrumphed and put down his accusatory finger. "I just want what's best for you."

"I think," Kitty replied, "you want what's best for you."

Brydon was jolted by her assertion and turned away. He sought comfort in contemplating a painting of a beautiful woman—somewhat older than Kitty, but with the same confidence around the eyes.

Kitty joined him. She knew that he sometimes felt as if he'd failed the memory of his wife, her mother, and been less than a perfect father. Kitty knew he'd done his best, and even as a little girl she'd always appreciated his efforts. "I'm sorry, Father," she said as she laid her hand on his arm.

"So am I," he said as he patted her hand. "My mistake was bringing you halfway across the world. Perhaps it would be best if you returned to England."

"England?" Kitty exclaimed, more than a little shocked. "But India is my home. I love it here." England was little more than a memory of waiting on a dock in a cold wet wind.

"You've grown into a beautiful young woman, Kitty. It's time you turned your mind to settling down."

"But, Father—"

He held up his hand. "I see no reason for you to stay here longer," he said. He looked at her with meaning. "Unless you've had a better offer? Hmm?"

She knew he was referring to Captain Boone.

Somehow, her heart did not sing at the thought of him, as it once had. Still, she did not want to go back to England.

"No, Father," Kitty said sadly.

Both of them were so involved with their own problems that neither of them noticed a figure crouching in the darkness on the ledge outside a window. It was Mowgli, of course, come for a last look at Kitty before he went to bed. He had heard most of the conversation, and realized its significance. Kitty would have to return to England unless she had a "better offer." Mowgli didn't know what a better offer might be, but he could not endure the thought of Kitty going away. He must do something to make her stay in India, to make her love him. Something civilized. That would be the hard part.

8

England or a "Better Offer"

Now this is the Law of the Jungle—as old and as
true as the sky;
And the wolf that shall keep it may prosper,
but the wolf that shall break it must die.
As the creeper that girdles the tree-trunk
the Law runneth forward and back—
For the strength of the pack is the wolf,
and the strength of the wolf is the pack.
—FROM THE JUNGLE LAW AS SPOKEN BY BALOO

Mowgli went into the jungle, where he picked
many of the red flowers. Afterward he took them
to Kitty's room while she slept and piled them all
around her.

"Fire," Mowgli whispered to himself over and

over again. "Fire." He imagined how happy Kitty would be when she awoke and saw all the flowers. She would know that he had been there, and that he loved her. She would not go to England.

He went downstairs to wait for her to get up. In one room he found an enormous painting of a person—man or woman he could not tell—with great masses of hair that flowed down his head and over his shoulders, strange trowsers that went only down to his knees, and shoes that had high platforms at the heels. Altogether, the picture was the strangest he had ever seen.

"King Louis of France," Kitty said as she walked up to him and contemplated the painting. "I'm sure one of the local servants hung it there to annoy us British." Kitty sounded more amused than annoyed.

"Looey, king of the Bandar-log." Mowgli nodded. "I know him. He lives in monkey city."

Kitty laughed. "I think not," she said.

"I have seen his hat. In monkey city, King Looey has one like it."

Kitty laughed again, but uneasily. Did some monkey king actually wear a crown like the one worn by King Louis of France? It seemed unlikely, but lately Kitty had learned that the most unlikely things were possible.

The native butler opened the door, allowing Captain Boone to enter with one hand behind his back. Mowgli growled.

"Mind your manners, Mowgli," Kitty said. "Hello, William. What a nice surprise."

Boone smiled, showing—as Mowgli thought— too many teeth. "We've both been so busy of late I thought I'd pay you a visit." With the flourish of a magician producing a rabbit from thin air, he brought three red flowers out from behind his back and offered them to Kitty.

"I know these are your favorite," Boone said.

Kitty wondered if he was being the least bit sarcastic, then decided to give him the benefit of the doubt. "Thank you, Billy. You're very sweet." She hugged him, then sat down with the flowers in her lap.

Boone sat down across from her and put one ankle across his knee. Mowgli sat down nearby and did the same, causing Boone to scowl. "Lessons going well, I hope," Boone said.

"Very well, thank you," Kitty said.

Boone uncrossed his legs, and Mowgli did the same.

England or a "Better Offer"

"Attentive, isn't he?" Boone asked, irritated. "A private moment, Kitty?" he asked as he stood. He offered his hand and Kitty took it. He led her out to the balcony and let the drapes drop behind them. When they were alone, he immediately sank to his knees. "Katherine Ann Brydon," he intoned with passion, "will you marry me?"

Kitty was astonished by Captain Boone's request. The truth was, whereas once she'd thought of nothing else but marrying him, lately she'd been preoccupied with other matters. "Well, I," Kitty began, still searching for the proper response, "I'm flattered."

"Good," Boone said as he got to his feet. "Then that's settled."

"But my father is planning to send me back to England, so I'm not sure—"

"Oh, don't worry about that, my darling. I've spoken to your father. He feels that this is—how did he put it?—a 'better offer.'" He grinned engagingly.

Kitty nodded as if she understood, which, in fact, she did. Like any good military tacticians, Captain Boone and her father had probably been plotting this proposal for days.

"I love you, Katherine." Boone kissed her

softly on the cheek and took both her hands in his. "We'll be the most perfect couple in all of India," he went on. "We'll have success, wealth, power—"

"And love."

"Of course. That goes without saying." He dropped her hands and turned away as if suddenly ashamed. "You know," he said as he turned to face her again, "I feel awful because I've been quite remiss in my duties to you of late." He brightened then and snapped his fingers. "I'll tell you what! Why don't I take your new friend—what's his name?"

"Mowgli." Why could no one but she remember his name?

"Mowgli. Yes, of course. Why don't I give Mowgli a tour of the palace. You'd like that, wouldn't you?"

"That would be very nice." She put her arm through his. "You know, Billy," she said as she walked him back into her room, "you can be quite sweet when you put your mind to it."

"Merely being polite, my darling."

Mowgli did not like Boone, and more than that, he did not trust him, but he agreed to the tour to please Kitty. Moreover, Boone continued to be pleasant, confusing Mowgli. What was this with man that one day he beat you and the next he took you on tours?

Boone took him to a room filled with daggers and rifles and other things with which men hurt each other.

"This is my favorite," Boone said as he removed a thick daggerlike thing from the wall. "It's a fifteenth-century knife. You see," he said as he plunged the knife into the air, "you thrust it into your opponent's belly"—he pushed a lever on the knife's handle, allowing serrated side blades to spring open—"then, when you pull it out, you rip out his guts." Boone twisted the knife and pulled it out. He smiled as he admired the weapon.

Mowgli was horrified. Could he have misunderstood? "Then you eat him?" he asked.

"No, of course not," Boone said, offended by the very thought.

"Does he want to eat you?"

"Why, no." Boone was confused by the question.

"Then why kill him?"

"Well, because he's your enemy."

"What is *enemy*?"

"Someone you hate." Boone disliked this line of questioning. He'd been a soldier all his life and such questions had never occurred to him. He put down the fifteenth-century knife, and from inside his tunic pulled something wrapped carefully in cloth. It was Mowgli's jeweled dagger.

Mowgli was surprised to see it, but he did not want it back—he'd not needed it lately.

"This belongs to you, doesn't it?"

"I found it," Mowgli said, which seemed to be a different thing altogether.

"Where did you find it?"

"In monkey city."

"Was there more treasure there?" Boone let the tips of his fingers polish the rubies and emeralds. "More of these shiny rocks?"

"Rubies and emeralds."

"Yes, yes. Rubies and emeralds."

"In monkey city there are mountains of them."

"Mountains?" Boone exclaimed. "I want you to take me to this monkey city."

"Only those who keep the Jungle Law may go." Mowgli no longer wanted to be in this room with these things that men used to kill when they were not hungry. And Boone's concern for these hard useless rocks made Mowgli uncomfortable.

"My dear boy," Boone explained, "I am a British officer. My *job* is to keep Her Majesty's law."

"Her Majesty's law is not Jungle Law."

"I don't know about any Jungle Law," Boone said, becoming irritated. "I keep man's law, and that's what counts around here."

"Jungle Law says we kill only to eat, or to keep from being eaten."

"Bravo," Boone said as he clapped his hands twice. "You almost sound like a man instead of like an animal that's been trained to sound like one."

Mowgli knew that Boone was trying to make him angry. He suspected it had something to do with the jewels, or with Kitty, or with both. The jewels did not matter, and surely Kitty would be able to chose between them. How would angering Mowgli help?

"The more I learn what is a man," Mowgli told him, "the more I want to be an animal."

"I *hunt* animals, you know," Boone said as he picked up a crossbow and aimed it at him.

He did not know what the British officer held

in his hands, but Mowgli assumed it was some sort of killing machine. It frightened him terribly, because to be killed by it would be to die without honor. Still, he did not believe Boone would use it here and now. "Maybe someday," Mowgli said, "you will hunt *me*."

"You have a talent for speaking the obvious," Boone said as he put down the crossbow. He nodded at Mowgli and went out. Mowgli knew that Boone was not finished asking him about monkey city. Next time he asked, Boone would certainly not be so polite.

❧ 9 ❧

The Divali Festival and After

The Divali Festival Dance was to take place a few weeks later, and everyone, even Captain Boone, was much busier than usual. Mowgli did not understand why everyone needed to work so hard to have fun, but he helped by doing whatever he could. Pleasing Kitty was his greatest joy.

On the night of the dance, the hundreds of lanterns that had been strung across the main courtyard of the palace glowed like fallen stars. Beneath them, men in dress uniforms, and women in flower-petal gowns browsed among long tables of food and drink. Natives of the highest caste had been invited, too—for instance, the Maharaja and Maharani who had lived in the palace before the British came. At one end of the courtyard was a large open space where couples danced to the music of an orchestra made up of native servants. A British officer stood in front of them waving a stick. Music was one of the few British things that Mowgli liked.

Mowgli tried to keep out of everyone's way. He was uncomfortable in the stiff British suit he wore. It itched, and squeezed him in the most unexpected places. His feet ached to be free of their shoes.

Dr. Plumford and his wife—a fat jovial woman—entered and the servant at the door bowed to them. "Mowgli," Plumford cried, and shook his hand. "You look splendid." He leaned close, as if telling Mowgli a secret. "Enjoy yourself, my boy. Here in this courtyard we have wine, women, and song—all the bare necessities!"

Not everyone was so friendly as Dr. Plumford. Boone and his friends made great sport of Mowgli, asking him to demonstrate how apes danced, or purposefully jostling him as they passed, saying, "Sorry, old man," and then giggling like Rose or Margaret.

Mowgli was thirsty and he thought he might

try the punch, though he would much have preferred water. Margaret and Alice stood nearby, watching him and laughing behind their fans. All right, the savage would give them a thrill. With one quick motion, he grabbed a fly that had been buzzing over the Yorkshire pudding. He brought the fly to his mouth and made large chewing motions while he smiled at Margaret and Alice. The young women went pale and hurried away. Mowgli chuckled as he opened his fist, releasing the fly unharmed.

His enjoyment did not last long, however, for he saw Kitty and Boone twirling gracefully across the dance floor. Even Mowgli had to admit they made a beautiful couple, and seeing them together made him sad.

When the dance was over, Boone excused himself and went to share some private joke with Wilkins and his other friends. Kitty headed for Margaret, Rose, and Alice.

Suddenly everything changed. The song that the orchestra began to play stirred a longing that Mowgli could hardly endure. He listened for a moment, trying to remember where he'd heard the song before. Then the answer jolted him. It was a waltz, the same waltz Kitty had danced to in her tent the night Shere Khan had come to the British camp, the night he had been saved by Raksha, the last night he had seen his father alive.

Kitty may have recognized the tune, too (as a matter of fact, years later she admitted to me that she had), because she approached Mowgli. "May I have this dance?" she asked.

"You may have it," Mowgli said, very pleased.

He swept her out onto the dance floor, where many other couples were already moving in three-quarter time. They danced to the center of the room, and the other couples spun around them.

One-two-three.

One-two-three.

Kitty smiled up at him, and Mowgli smiled down at her. They took joy from moving together as one. Neither of them even considered the possibility that Captain Boone might be watching them and not liking what he saw. It was perfect, it was magical—the evening, the dance, the people. Then the waltz was over, and the couples applauded themselves—Mowgli a little louder than the others, it was true, but not so loud as to be crude.

The Divali Festival and After

Colonel Brydon marched up and stood in front of the orchestra. He lifted his hands, quieting the crowd, smiling all the while with some secret knowledge. Kitty moved up to join him.

"Thank you one and all," he said, "for attending this year's Divali Festival Dance."

More applause. Colonel Brydon waited for it to end.

"I would especially like to thank the Maharaja and Maharani for the continued use of their lovely palace."

More applause. I can tell you now, O best beloved, that the Maharaja and Maharani had no choice about who used their palace. It was easier to loan the palace to the British than it was to fight them, for at that time the British Empire controlled one of the most powerful armies on earth.

"And now," Colonel Brydon went on, "I have an announcement to make." He fairly beamed. "One of the finest young men I've ever had the privilege to know has sought my consent to marry my daughter, Katherine, she having accepted his proposal."

Kitty had no idea this announcement was to be made, and she stood in the expectant silence, shocked. She could not have been more confused and upset if the courtyard had suddenly gone upside down.

"Never having been one to stand in the way of progress—or true love—I am delighted to give them my consent."

The members of the crowd showed their approval by applauding more wildly than they had before that evening. Kitty felt only as if she were trapped. She tried to smile.

"So," Colonel Brydon said, oblivious to his daughter's discomfort, "it gives me the greatest pleasure to announce the engagement of Katherine Ann Brydon to Captain William Boone. A toast." As if by magic, a servant appeared from nowhere with a glass of champagne. Similar feats happened all over the courtyard. Soon everyone had a glass and was raising it in the direction of the stage.

Boone stepped forward to slip a diamond ring onto Kitty's finger. She let him do it, but she felt nothing. The shock had numbed her.

"Here, here," came the cry from all over the courtyard.

The orchestra struck up another waltz, and Boone and Kitty began to dance. Soon they were surrounded by happy couples, all glowing with the knowledge that they had just witnessed a special moment.

Mowgli and the Plumfords stood in a far corner of the courtyard. Dr. Plumford seemed as stunned as Kitty. Mowgli knew something bad had just happened, but he could not imagine what. "What does it mean, Doctor?" Mowgli asked.

"It means the two of them are to be wed," Plumford said sadly. "It means she belongs to him."

This British thing was even worse than Mowgli had feared. *It means she belongs to him.*

Mowgli no longer had any heart for a party. He walked toward the door, and Wilkins bumped into him hard. "Sorry, old bean," Wilkins said. Immediately he was gone, another soldier poked his elbow into Mowgli's side. "Dreadfully sorry, old chap."

It seemed that the entire British army bumped him and jostled him, each time apologizing. Mowgli grew angry, but like the Maharaja, he didn't want to fight the British. He just wanted to be left alone.

Then Wilkins was there again. He grinned in

the most awful way and pushed Mowgli. He fell backward, trying to regain his balance, and crashed into one of the food-laden tables. Food, drink, utensils, Mowgli, all fell to the floor together in a heap.

The orchestra stopped. All eyes glared at Mowgli with distaste. A few soldiers could not hold in their laughter. No jungle beast was ever so cruel. Mowgli did not know how to defend himself against laughter and stares. He could only go away, back to where he knew and understood his enemies, back to where he could find comfort. He stood up, flung the worst of the mess from his suit, and ran out of the courtyard.

Kitty, seeing that Boone was enjoying Mowgli's humiliation, could no longer bear to be with him. She ran after Mowgli.

"Let him go," Boone cried after her, but she would not stop. Mowgli needed her.

Kitty followed a trail of soiled clothing to a parapet, where she found Mowgli about to leap over the side into the jungle. "Mowgli," she cried.

He froze and turned to face her. Even now he could not ignore her.

"Where are you going?" she asked.

"I go home to the jungle."

"You are not an animal," she insisted. "You are a man. You must live among men."

"I am not a man!" Mowgli cried, and for the first time felt the sadness of that statement; he had known for a long time that he was not a creature of the jungle either. He did not know what he was, but he knew that he did not belong here. The Jungle Laws were *his* laws, even if he did not belong in the jungle. "I run with the wolf pack," he said, almost whispering.

Kitty just looked at him, her eyes glistening with tears.

"You must run with the man pack," Mowgli explained. "It is the proper and civilized thing."

Boone stepped onto the parapet and took stock of the scene.

"I will shame your house no more," Mowgli said, and dropped over the parapet. In a few seconds he was running into the jungle, and thereby missed a conversation that might have pleased him, if anything could.

Boone took a few steps to stand directly behind Kitty. It disturbed him that she stared out into the darkness with such yearning. "Katherine, I think you owe me an apology."

She turned slowly and saw his angry face. She was very tired, but this one last battle must be fought. "There's been a mistake, William," she said.

"A mistake?" Boone asked, disbelieving.

"I can't marry you. I won't marry you."

"No, Kat, I think it is you who is mistaken."

Though he did not move, he frightened her. The very look in his eyes seemed threatening.

"I realize," he went on coolly, "the adolescent infatuation you have with that savage has addled your brain." He grabbed her wrist and held on so tightly that he hurt her. She did not cry out. She would not. "But I cannot allow you to make a fool of *me,* Katherine. And I will not lose you to some jungle boy!"

She pulled away and slapped him hard. For a moment they glared at each other. Boone suddenly turned and walked away, leaving Kitty to stare out at the jungle. Its huge darkness spread to the horizon. Boone would not dare hurt her, but he was also not the sort to let an insult rest. Mowgli was certainly in great danger, and she had no idea how to help him.

• • •

The Divali Festival and After

Still miserable, Mowgli came to a clearing and sat down. He pulled off the trowsers and hung them like a flag from a convenient bush. He was not an animal, but if Boone was any sample, he was not a man either. He was just Mowgli.

Baloo came along to see how he was, and this gave Mowgli an idea. "One-two-three, one-two-three," Mowgli sang as he tried to make Baloo dance a waltz. "Clumsy Baloo," Mowgli said affectionately. They danced until Baloo could no longer stand it. That was all right with Mowgli. Baloo did not dance like Kitty anyway.

Much later that night, after the food was all eaten and the last dance was played, while Colonel Brydon and Kitty each tossed in their separate beds, Boone and Wilkins kept an appointment at the Black Raven Tavern, a pub of bad repute in the worst part of Waingara village.

The Black Raven was a hive of scum and villainy. Men who traded in death and stolen goods drank, gambled, and caroused with the women who preyed upon such men. It was a dirty noisy place that would have been smoky from the tobacco and more exotic substances in use there, if it were not for the fact that the tavern had no roof but the sky. Frequent fights broke out—over women, or games of chance, or a fair trade of goods or services—but participants were hustled out into the alley before they could harm business.

Boone and Wilkins entered this place wearing civilian clothes, but still acutely aware of how out of place they were. They found Buldeo and Tabaqui at a balcony table and sat down.

"Drinks for my friends," Buldeo cried to the world at large, and snapped his fingers.

"With friends like us," Boone said, smiling his most charming smile, "you may not need enemies."

"That is good," Buldeo said, "because I am having plenty of those. May I be seeing the dagger?" He held out his hand. It was hard and lined and none too clean.

Wilkins was surprised at the question. "What makes you think we brought it?" he asked.

"Such an object would not be leaving my possession," Buldeo said.

Boone laughed and pulled the dagger from his vest. He unwrapped the cloth from it and handed the weapon to Buldeo, who turned it over, studying it. Even in the dim light of the Black Raven, the jewels in the monkey-and-python device glittered.

Like Buldeo, Tabaqui was entranced by the dagger and what it represented. "You see, sahibs," Tabaqui said, "the lost city of Hanuman is no legend."

"Tell on," Wilkins said,

"Two thousand years ago," Buldeo said, falling into the cadences of a storyteller, "in the time of Hanuman, deep in the thickest heart of the dark jungle, was built a city of most surpassing magnificence. All peoples of Asia are traveling there, hoping for a chance to save their souls."

"Bought their way into Heaven, did they?" Boone suggested, leering.

"Indeed, sahib. And the treasures, they are piling higher and higher, until one day, the jungle is becoming angry and swallowing the city whole."

The four men at the table contemplated the dagger before them and the jungle outside the walls of Waingara village.

"To go into the black jungle," Tabaqui said, "is to invite death."

"Unless one is knowing the way," Buldeo said.

"The jungle boy," Wilkins said.

"Precisely," Boone said. He took the dagger away from Buldeo, carefully wrapped it, and hid it again in his vest. "But getting Mowgli's cooperation will take some—how to put this delicately?—persuasion."

Buldeo and Tabaqui grinned unpleasantly at each other, showing many rotted teeth. "Have no fear, sahib," Buldeo said. "I am having all the persuasion you need."

Boone and Wilkins nodded.

~ 10 ~

Treachery on the Jaipur Road

Kitty, Boone, and Wilkins set off at the same time—Kitty bound for England, Boone and Wilkins bound for the great Indian jungle.

Mowgli had no idea that anyone was out to capture him. He thought that since he had finished with the British, the British were finished with him as well. But a strange smell awakened him from a dream of Kitty, and he followed it down to a path where he saw Sergeant Harley sneaking along with a butterfly net at the ready. Boone and Wilkins followed on horses and searched from side to side from their high vantage point.

Mowgli was puzzled by all this activity and

didn't see how it could have anything to do with him until Tabaqui suddenly ran at him with a net of his own. Mowgli had only just flung off Tabaqui when Sergeant Harley ran at him swinging the butt of a rifle. Mowgli kicked him as he had earlier in the dungeon. This put Harley out of commission, but Tabaqui had had enough time to recover, and he ran at Mowgli again. Mowgli had quickly tired of this game. He threw dirt into Tabaqui's face and ran.

He had not gone far when he heard the thunder of a rifle firing twice. Not even an Englishman fired without a reason. Fearful of what it might mean, Mowgli quickly ran back to the site of his battle with Tabaqui and Harley. He found Baloo lying in the clearing with blood on his chest. He was alive, but he groaned in a heartrending way that caused Mowgli to worry for his life.

"Oh, my poor silly Baloo," Mowgli whispered as he cradled the bear's head in his arms. He knew what he must do. After making Baloo as comfortable as possible, he called Bagheera and Gray Brother and the wolf pack, and ran for all he was worth to Waingara Palace.

When he arrived, he quickly made his way to

the quarters Colonel Brydon shared with Kitty. After a little searching, he found the native butler who had been so patient teaching him how to use a knife and fork.

The butler seemed surprised and frightened to see him, but he managed to blurt out that Dr. Plumford was no longer in the palace, having joined Colonel Brydon escorting Kitty to the England boat. They had taken the Jaipur road.

Before the echo of the butler's voice had fallen, Mowgli was gone.

He ran down the Jaipur road with Bagheera, Gray Brother, and the pack. Not knowing where on the road Kitty was, Mowgli dared not take any shortcuts to Jaipur. He and his friends went as swiftly as jungle creatures can.

When Mowgli came upon the carriage, Buldeo, Tabaqui, and a gang of men who looked even dirtier and more fierce were attacking. Dead and wounded soldiers lay all about, as well as a few of the gang. Kitty stood in the carriage not knowing what to do and very frightened. Her father was nowhere to be seen, and Buldeo was about to plunge a knife into Dr. Plumford, who had fallen out of the carriage to the ground.

Mowgli leapt at Buldeo, knocking him away

from Dr. Plumford, and they rolled in the dust. He was surprised when Buldeo smiled at him. Bagheera lashed about at some of the gang, and the wolf pack ran off the rest.

Tabaqui trotted up on his big horse, grabbed the reins of the carriage horses, and with a cry led them down the road at a furious clip that caused Kitty to fall back into her seat.

Buldeo pushed Mowgli away and escaped into the jungle where the rest of his gang had gone. Mowgli ran to see if Dr. Plumford was all right.

"They took Katherine and the colonel," Plumford gasped, trying to catch his breath. "Why?"

"They want me to come for her," Mowgli said as he glared into the jungle. Bagheera and the pack prowled up and down the road a ways, sniffing at the dead. "They *know* I will come for her."

"They are dangerous men, Mowgli."

"All men are dangerous," Mowgli said as he pulled Plumford to his feet.

"You saved my life, Mowgli. Thank you."

"Yes, Doctor. And now I need you to save the life of another."

Plumford looked puzzled, but that would not

last long. Mowgli knew that Kitty would be safe, at least until he arrived. For the moment Baloo's need was greater.

Keeping a mad pace, Tabaqui led the wagon to the bamboo bridge where Kitty had first met Mowgli what seemed a very long time ago. Buldeo was already there. Tabaqui pulled Kitty from the carriage. She backed away from him and ran into Sergeant Harley.

"Nice day for it, miss," he said, and saluted her with his rifle.

Whose side was he on?

Boone and Wilkins walked over to her, and for a moment she thought that she and her father were saved.

"Hello, Kat," Boone said as if they were meeting for croquet. "It appears that I get the last dance after all."

Kitty could do nothing but stare at him, too stunned even to be afraid. Back in the carriage, she heard groans, and she turned to see her father struggling to get up on the seat.

"Captain Boone," he said. "Thank God."

Boone looked at Buldeo. "Why did you bring

him here?" he asked angrily. "That wasn't part of the plan."

"God's holey trowsers," Colonel Brydon exclaimed. He was not given to using profanity, O best beloved, but truth to tell, he had never before been so astonished. "You're with these, these creatures?"

"Much to my surprise," Boone said, smiling, "I have many friends in low places." He inclined his head slightly making a mocking bow.

"You are an officer in the British army," Brydon cried. "Return us to the palace. That is a direct order!"

Boone chuckled as if Brydon had just told a joke. "Of course. Back to the palace, where I will be hanged, drawn, and quartered. No thank you."

"This is treason! I order you to—"

Boone nodded and Tabaqui struck Colonel Brydon in the side of the head with a rifle butt. Kitty screamed as her father fell back to the floor of the carriage. She went to him, then looked up at Boone.

"Why are we here?" she asked. She had never hated a person so much.

"I am the reason," Mowgli said as he stepped into view on a tree limb.

Treachery on the Jaipur Road

Everyone looked up at him.

"Right on schedule," Wilkins commented approvingly.

Buldeo grabbed Kitty and twisted her arm behind her while he held the jeweled dagger to her throat.

"If you are a good jungle boy and take us to the treasure, I will let her live," Boone said.

"Don't do it, Mowgli," Kitty cried.

"Quiet," Buldeo said, and gave her arm another twist.

"I will take you there," Mowgli said. "We will see who lives."

Nearby, Bagheera growled. Boone and his men looked around nervously, but Mowgli only smiled. "We will see," he said again.

Mowgli allowed his hands to be tied, and like a dog on a leash, he led Boone and his people through the jungle. Kitty helped her father limp along as best he could on his injured leg. Mowgli could see that all this walking did him no good.

Boone tried to explain to Colonel Brydon why he wanted the treasure. "I wasn't given everything," he said, "like some people." He nodded meaningfully at Kitty and her father. "Now I want mine."

Wilkins walked along with Mowgli, the rope wrapped around his wrist. "You don't want the treasure," Wilkins said. "Why be difficult?"

"If you find the treasure, more men will come."

"And when men from outside enter the jungle," Brydon said between winces of pain, "it is always bad for those who live there. Your father told me that, Mowgli."

His father? Colonel Brydon could not mean Father Wolf, Raksha's husband. He must mean a man, someone Mowgli remembered only dimly. His man-father must have been very wise.

If they chose, animals can make much noise as they run through the jungle—so as not to surprise a friend, or to frighten prey. Now they were most noisy indeed.

"It is said," Buldeo began in his storyteller rhythm, "that no jungle animal will harm the jungle boy, and that they will rise up to help him."

Mowgli looked upward, and Boone followed his gaze. He stopped, stiff with fear. Bagheera rested on a tree limb above them, his eyes narrow.

"Why does he stare at us like that?" Boone asked.

"Because," Mowgli said, "to him, you are food."

Boone shuddered, putting on bravery like a suit of clothes. He pushed Mowgli onward and trotted quickly under Bagheera, not even daring to slow down to aim his rifle.

Colonel Brydon's injury became worse. He shivered though his body was very hot. Kitty demanded that Boone allow Mowgli to lead them back to the palace, where a doctor could be found. Boone ignored her—his only concern was getting to the monkey city.

Boone ordered that camp be made. Sergeant Harley whistled as he scurried around making preparations with the sluggish help of Tabaqui. The wolves began to howl at sunset, comforting only Mowgli. Kitty and her father bore the cries well, but more than once Wilkins threw something at the black wall of jungle around them and demanded Mowgli make the wolves stop.

"A man talking to animals?" Mowgli asked, playing dumb. "Is this done?"

Boone, Buldeo, and Tabaqui became more nervous as time passed, but wolves did not seem to bother Harley. Apparently he could sleep through anything.

Much later Mowgli howled in answer, and the howling of the pack stopped. "What's that?" Harley asked. He sat up and looked around.

The sudden silence was complete, as if the jungle were empty of all life but the small party going to monkey city.

Something roared nearby. The sound was unforgiving and full of anger. Boone and Wilkins leapt to their feet, their weapons ready.

"What was that?" Wilkins whispered as he scanned the darkness.

Buldeo was still sitting, but his knuckles showed white against the rifle in his hand. "Shere Khan," he said. "He has returned."

"I'd like to get me a tiger," Boone said, smiling at the thought.

"Do not wish for this tiger, sahib," Buldeo warned.

"Shere Khan protects the creatures of the jungle," Mowgli said.

They turned to him as if they'd forgotten he was there. He stood in a patch of moonlight, looking like the spirit of the jungle despite the fact that his hands were still tied behind his back.

Treachery on the Jaipur Road

"Shere Khan keeps the Jungle Law," Mowgli went on. "Those who break it do so at their peril."

"Shere Khan killed your father," Buldeo said.

"No, it was *you,* Buldeo," Colonel Brydon said. He was sweating badly, and he seemed thin and weak. Kitty watched him with concern. "*You* killed Mowgli's father with your cowardice."

Mowgli was surprised by Colonel Brydon's words, but he did not doubt them. He glared at Buldeo. Buldeo stared back for a moment, then hefted his rifle and walked farther along the path till he was out of sight.

"Go back to sleep," Boone commanded. "Another long day tomorrow." He sat down and rolled himself up in a blanket.

Shere Khan did not roar again for a long time. Mowgli crept over to Kitty and Colonel Brydon. Wilkins stirred, but he kept his grip on the rope. "Shere Khan hunts us," Mowgli said. "I must escape."

"We're going with you," Kitty said. She looked at her father worriedly.

"You must not," Mowgli said. "For now, you will be safer with these men and their guns." He nodded in the direction of Boone and his men.

"Only when they find monkey city will they kill you. I will not allow this to happen."

"I know," Kitty said confidently.

They stared into each other's eyes for a moment, then Mowgli went a few feet away and waited patiently by himself. Just before dawn, Bagheera crept out of the jungle so silently that even Mowgli barely heard him. Bagheera chewed on the rope binding Mowgli. He felt the big cat's teeth and raspy tongue and knew that he would soon be free.

Harley turned onto his back and coughed like a man about to awaken. Mowgli knew he must escape now. He flexed his hands against the weakened rope and it broke easily. As he ran into the jungle he heard Harley sounding the alarm.

Gray Brother led a few wolves back along the path to discourage pursuers. Meanwhile Mowgli drew an arrow in the dirt, showing the way to monkey city. He hoped that would satisfy Boone for the moment. Mowgli was far away when he heard a scream of terror.

When he saw Harley sinking into the quicksand, Wilkins was already too late. He desperately held out his rifle to Harley, and Harley tried time and again to grasp it. But either his hands were too slippery, or he was too frightened, or he had already sunk too deeply—in any case, he soon sank out of sight, leaving no mark. Wilkins stared at the pool of quicksand, unable to believe what had just happened.

Boone and Buldeo ran up with the backpacks while Tabaqui roughly pushed Kitty forward.

"He's gone," Wilkins said.

"Well," Boone said cheerfully, "we can't be discouraged by every little thing."

"Looks like your knight in shinning armor has deserted you, Princess," Wilkins said to Kitty, but nastily.

"I think not," Boone said. He pointed with his rifle at the arrow Mowgli had drawn in the dirt.

Shere Khan roared, and the sound seemed to echo through the whole jungle.

"Let's go," Boone said as he slid a bullet into the chamber of his rifle. He walked off, and Tabaqui had to half drag Kitty after him.

"But my father!" Kitty cried. "We can't leave him! He'll die!"

"Such is life," Boone said, and kept walking.

• • •

Mowgli collected a few friends, then circled around and came back to find Colonel Brydon pulling himself along the path back to the palace. At the rate he was going, he would be at it for years. He did not have years. Mowgli judged that without help, Colonel Brydon would be dead in a few hours at most.

Brydon was most grateful for Mowgli's help and, in return, asked only that Mowgli rescue Kitty. "I'm sorry that I misjudged you, Mowgli. It is obvious to me now that one does not recognize a savage by the clothes he wears or by his abilities with a knife and fork."

Mowgli graciously forgave him everything, then loaded him onto an elephant and told the elephant to take his passenger to the man-village at Waingara.

Mowgli tore a patch from Brydon's uniform. "For your daughter," he said, and Brydon nodded.

When Colonel Brydon and the elephant had disappeared among the trees, Mowgli climbed aboard a second elephant. "Tut-tut-tut," he said, and the elephant walked into the jungle in the other direction.

Treachery on the Jaipur Road

So it happened that while Wilkins and Tabaqui hacked their way through the jungle, sweating and cursing, Mowgli followed them in comfort atop his elephant. He drew arrows in the dirt every few miles so that Boone would know he was still around. Once, he left an arrow of red flowers and the patch from Colonel Brydon's uniform so that Kitty would know her father was safe and under Mowgli's protection.

Mowgli had no trouble following Boone. The British left footprints and many broken branches. They made more noise than a herd of elephants. He was watching them from the top of a cliff when Tabaqui leapt out at him and pushed him to the ground.

"Like you," Tabaqui said, "I am a hunter. I know to stay downwind."

Mowgli jumped to his feet; he and Tabaqui circled each other like wrestlers. Suddenly they were on each other with fists and nails. They rolled around on the ground, and for a moment Tabaqui strangled Mowgli over the edge of the cliff. Under his head was nothing but the sharp rocks hundreds of feet below. Mowgli used his feet to push him off and got a short rest. But Tabaqui continued to come at him, punching again and again, till Mowgli was cross-eyed with pain and confusion. He sank to his knees.

Tabaqui smiled and lifted a great rock over his head, intending to bash Mowgli's head in. Mowgli blinked at the silhouette standing over him and gave it a small shove. The rock unbalanced Tabaqui. He called for help as he stumbled backward, but Mowgli was in no condition to help if he'd wanted to. The rock pulled Tabaqui over the edge. He screamed as he fell. Mowgli passed out before the scream stopped abruptly.

Miles away, Boone, Wilkins, and Buldeo heard the scream, and they discussed whether Tabaqui had in fact killed Mowgli. Boone was not sure who had killed whom, and thought it wiser not to assume too much. He pushed Kitty forward.

Later that day they crossed a river below a high waterfall that thundered and foamed and made rainbows in its mist. Kitty looked up at the fall and saw Mowgli watching from a thick branch that projected from its side. She called out his name. Her cry echoed over and over until a thousand Kittys seemed to have cried out.

"It can't be," Wilkins said as he and Buldeo raised their rifles. They fired again and again as

Treachery on the Jaipur Road

Mowgli dropped out of sight among the great clouds of mist. Kitty could not tell whether he had jumped or fallen. She could not tell whether he had been hit. All she knew was that nothing surfaced in the pool below the falls. Nothing at all.

🙟 11 🙟

Good Hunting

The jungle suddenly ended at a high stone wall. Buldeo and Wilkins stumbled forward still swinging their machetes as if by reflex. Boone entered the clearing with Kitty. The four stood in awe.

The wall was carved with gigantic representations of the city dwellers, who obviously believed themselves to be bold, intelligent, and beautiful, the chosen of their gods. The wall was cracked and weathered, but still formidable. Vines crawled over it like sleeping snakes. As high as the wall was, the spires of the ancient city towered above it.

"God's holey trowsers, we found it," Boone said, feeling some disbelief.

"Hanuman," Buldeo agreed.

Something in the jungle roared. It was very close, and it frightened them badly.

"Shere Khan," Buldeo said as he looked around.

The roar stopped, and now they could hear insane chattering from beyond the wall as thousands of Bandar-log sought cover. Mowgli had warned them, after all, that Hanuman was now a city of monkeys.

They all backed away from the wall and the screaming monkeys beyond. Suddenly a shape in black and white and orange leapt from the jungle, raking Buldeo's shoulder before he managed to get a shot off at it.

"Shere Khan is mine," Buldeo said, and ran into the jungle after the tiger.

Boone pulled Kitty along the wall, looking for a way into the city. Wilkins followed slowly, terrified of staying outside with the jungle's protector, and just as terrified of going inside where thousands of wild monkeys dwelled.

"Come on, Wilkins," Boone cried. "I've found the entrance." Indeed, he and Kitty entered the courtyard and approached the great monkey-head statue. They heard a roar, then a terrible scream.

"Wilkins?" Boone cried.

Only silence answered him.

"One more down," Kitty said. She had no fear of Shere Khan. Mowgli would protect her.

"More treasure for me," Boone said as he shrugged.

Kitty could not help being intrigued by the old city for it was full of mystery. She cared little for treasure, but the opportunity to learn the secrets of the people who had built the city lured her. She and Boone used a ladder of vines and cracks in the monkey statue to climb to its mouth. Breathless, they pushed spiderwebs aside as they walked through the tunnel that led to the plaza.

They stopped when they came into the sunlight again and stared across the empty plaza at the palace. Silence fell onto them like a heavy cloak. Where were the monkeys?

An orangutan, looking ridiculous in mismatched clothing and a crown of more-than-Oriental splendor, waddled out through a doorway and made a rude noise at them. Kitty almost laughed.

Good Ijunting

"See?" Mowgli said.

Boone and Kitty turned and saw him leaning casually against a gigantic stone python.

"I told you," Mowgli said. "King Looey!"

Boone fired, and Mowgli ducked behind the python. The bullet ricocheted off the stone block where Mowgli had been. He glanced out again. "Follow him. He will guide you to the treasure."

King Looey jumped up and down and went inside. Boone grabbed Kitty roughly by the arm and dragged her with him as he followed.

Boone and Kitty stepped into darkness. Near the door, they found a torch that Boone lit with a safety match. In the flickering light, they saw King Looey waddling through another doorway. They followed him cautiously and came into an enormous room in which liquid dripped. By the light of the torch, Boone saw an aqueduct that ran around the room at shoulder height. He tasted the liquid on one finger and smiled. "Absolutely brilliant," he said as he touched the stuff in the aqueduct with his torch.

Immediately, the fire spread along the aqueduct, came to a place where it divided, and then ran out in may directions; it divided again and again, until the entire palace was illuminated by the oil in the aqueducts. Boone threw his torch aside and Kitty slapped him as hard as she could. Boone only laughed and pulled her along after King Looey.

While Boone was discovering the secret of illuminating the palace, Mowgli crept in. He followed Boone and Kitty by the sounds they made. Suddenly fire sprang up all round him, and he saw that he was in a long room with fireplaces down one side. Pots and pans still hung from the opposite wall. This was certainly what the British called a kitchen. Through the doorway, Mowgli saw Boone pulling Kitty along a cross hallway. He ran after them, but was stopped when somebody fired at him. He hid behind the angle of a wall. He peaked out and saw Buldeo leveling his rifle at him again. Mowgli ran.

He led Buldeo through rooms and hallways in the lower levels of the palace. Now and again Buldeo squeezed off a shot. Once, the bullet came close enough that Mowgli felt the grit kicked off the wall when it struck.

Mowgli ran into an enormous room and barely skidded to a stop on the marble floor before he fell into the large square pit in the center of it. The pit was large enough to accommodate a small herd of elephants, but it contained only an enormous box covered in the precious rocks. A fantastically carved roof was held above it by many smooth columns.

Mowgli didn't know it till Dr. Plumford explained later, but this was a mausoleum, a place where the dead were kept. The box was a coffin. Judging by the trouble that had been taken with the burial arrangements, these were royal dead.

Mowgli leapt into the pit as Buldeo fired at him again. "I know you're down there, man-cub," Buldeo cried, and leapt into the pit after him.

They circled the enormous marble coffin, keeping it between them. Mowgli ran around to approach Buldeo from behind. Buldeo turned suddenly and fired. Mowgli ducked out of the way and the bullet struck the ceramic head of a monkey that laughed upon the wall. The monkey head shattered like a broken pot, allowing sand to begin pouring into the pit.

Slowly, with an eerie silence, the columns began to sink into the floor, lowering the heavy marble roof.

Buldeo paid no attention to the roof, but continued to stalk Mowgli. He heard a sound and turned to fire. As he did so he was knocked off balance when the sand streamed out of another ceramic monkey head. More sand fell into the pit. The level of the sand rose, and the marble roof came down more quickly.

At last Buldeo noticed that he was in danger of being buried alive. Already, wading through the sand was difficult. Mowgli climbed him as if Buldeo were a tree, and leapt from his shoulders to the top of the coffin. Buldeo could not shoot because his gun was lost somewhere in the sand.

The space between the roof and the floor was very narrow and getting smaller as Mowgli watched. He leapt from the coffin and managed to roll under the roof just before it settled into place, cutting off Buldeo's anguished cry for help.

Mowgli breathed hard as he stared at the roof, now covering the hole in the floor. Buldeo had been a bad man, but Mowgli was sorry he had died in such a terrible way.

A slap echoed through the palace.

"If you hit me again, I'll—" Boone managed to say before Kitty slapped him again.

Mowgli followed the sounds of argument to another room—this one smaller than the others, and without decoration. He arrived just in time to see Boone strike Kitty with the butt of his pistol. She slumped against him, unconscious.

"No!" Mowgli cried.

Boone fired at him, but the pistol clicked time after time. He was out of ammunition. Suddenly frightened, he backed away from Mowgli, pulling Kitty with him. He reached backward with a foot and, still gripping Kitty, fell through a square hole. Mowgli dropped down the hole after them.

He fell into the treasure chamber, now awash with light from the fire in the aqueduct. His eyes found no rest. Everything sparkled and gleamed. Kitty lay nearby. He went to her and saw that she was still alive. Where was Boone?

Mowgli searched the room. Suddenly a sea of jewels rattled like gravel as the giant golden elephant statue fell forward. Mowgli moved out of the way just in time as the thing crashed into the jewels and revealed Boone with sword in hand, ready for a fight.

Mowgli looked around for a weapon and picked up a dagger much like the one he'd found on his previous visit to the treasure room. Boone stepped forward quickly and slashed at him.

That was the start of an amazing fight. And except for Boone and Mowgli, the only ones who saw it were the Bandar-log, the Monkey-People who lived in the city. Up and back the combatants went across the gold and jewels, slashing and parrying and slashing again. Boone was more skilled with a blade, but he was distracted by the cries and posturing of the Bandar-log. Mowgli's concentration was better. He was also more energetic and graceful—and he was fighting for his life, not just for treasure.

"What is it you think you have that I don't?" Boone asked as he struck at Mowgli again and again.

Mowgli used his dagger to block the attacks. He noticed a hump moving under the piles of treasure and knew that they had attracted the attention of Kaa, the great snake that guarded the treasure room. They needed to end this brawl or they would both die.

"I have feet in the jungle that leave no mark," Mowgli said. "Eyes that see in the dark. Ears that hear the smallest bark." He lashed out with his dagger and cut Boone's sword arm. The Englishman dropped his sword and stared at Mowgli, astonished. "And sharp, white teeth," Mowgli concluded. Kaa was getting closer.

He ran to Kitty. Still half-unconcious, she punched with her fist. Only when Mowgli caught the punch in his hand did she awaken entirely and smile at him. "Come," he said. "We must go quickly." He pulled her to her feet and led her across the golden plain.

"But we must take some of the treasure home!" Kitty cried. "Look at it!"

Mowgli stopped to regard her sadly. "You cannot eat it," he said. "And it cannot love you. What good is it?"

"But it's a fortune," Kitty exclaimed. "It can buy you, well, it can buy you—"

"Happiness? Love? Friends?" He shook his head. "This treasure brings only death. Leave it to the monkeys. They, too, like pretty bright things."

Kitty sighed, but she went willingly with Mowgli. They passed Boone, who was on his knees, filling his backpack with coins, diamonds, and strands of pearls. "Go," he cried. "I have what I came for!"

Mowgli saw Kaa approaching under the treasure, and he took Kitty away quickly. They had escaped Kaa, but he didn't think that Boone would.

And indeed, best beloved, Boone continued to load his backpack until he could barely lift it. He carried it across the moat on the small bridge, but as he reached the other side something grabbed him around the ankle. He screamed as it pulled him into the water. Boone fought bravely, but the treasure weighed him down. By the time he thought to unstrap the backpack, it was too late for him. The water in the moat churned and bubbled as Kaa took the latest in an endless chain of treasure hunters.

Mowgli and Kitty were crossing the plaza when they heard Boone's scream rise from the well. "He is Kaa's now," Mowgli said as Kitty turned to bury her face in his chest.

They went to the tunnel that would lead out through the open mouth of the monkey, but someone was waiting for them there. It was Shere Khan.

❦ 12 ❦

Man Goes to Man

Mowgli stepped in front of Kitty and held his dagger ready. Shere Khan did not move, but only roared at them. Mowgli thought he had never heard anything so loud and frightening—so different from the friendly growl of Bagheera.

What to do? Mowgli felt as if he were facing not just a tiger, but his destiny. Was he brave enough to confront it? He could see no choice. It was either face the tiger or live forever in fear.

Mowgli walked forward and crouched so that he could look Shere Khan in the face, eye to eye. Shere Khan roared again. Instead of shying away, Mowgli roared back at him.

Shere Khan seemed surprised. He sat down and gave a warm growl back in his inside cupboards.

"What happened?" Kitty asked.

"Shere Khan sees me not as a man, but as a jungle creature." He stuck his dagger into his waistband. "Truly, there is honor among tigers."

Suddenly a wind came up, shaking the trees, so that their leaves made the sound of a million insects. Then a single musical note chimed. Mowgli and Kitty looked all around and could not determine its source. It seemed to come from everywhere.

When they looked back at the entrance to the tunnel, Shere Khan was gone and an old man was standing exactly where the tiger had been. He was an ancient holy man in clean white robes. Kitty had no idea what was going on, but she knew that she was seeing something quite extraordinary—perhaps even supernatural. She tingled with excitement.

The holy man and Mowgli traded smiles. The holy man put his hands together and bowed to Mowgli. Mowgli put his hands together and returned the bow. Kitty did the same. They came up from their bows and found that the old man had vanished along with the big tiger. The tunnel was open, and led home.

Mowgli and Kitty held each other for a long time.

Mowgli and Kitty returned to the bamboo bridge where they had first met. Bagheera and Gray Brother and all the pack ran with them, and it was a joyous running.

Colonel Brydon and a troop of soldiers waited across the bridge. He wore bandages on his leg, but he was much better, and would certainly recover. A wiser man for his adventures, he crisply saluted Mowgli and his friends.

Baloo had clean bandages across his chest. He sat next to Dr. Plumford, who, amazingly, seemed perfectly comfortable resting his hand on Baloo's shoulder.

And, O best beloved, that is how it came to pass that Mowgli, keeper of the Jungle Law, protector of the jungle's creatures, became lord of the jungle.

Like Mowgli, I wish good hunting to you and to all who keep the Jungle Law!

• • •

Man goes to Man! Cry the challenge through the jungle!
He that was our brother goes away. . .
Man goes to Man! (Oh, we loved him in the jungle!)
To the man-trail where we may not follow more.